"I'm sorry."

"Don't you dare apologize," Rocco said.

Mercy pressed a hand to her clammy forehead. "I don't know what happened."

"I think I do. You had a panic attack. Have there been any big changes in your life? Anything different going on to cause you anxiety?"

Panic attack?

Sometimes it was hard to breathe because her very existence was shrinking under her father's thumb. But this was the first time she had manifested any physical symptoms.

"This is my last training session." Dread bubbled inside her, the thought of not having any future sessions with *him* unbearable. "My father won't allow me to come back."

"Why not?"

"It doesn't matter." Tears pricked her eyes that she refused to shed. "The point is I won't be able to see you anymore."

WYOMING COWBOY UNDERCOVER

JUNO RUSHDAN

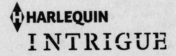

HARLEQUIN
INTRIGUE

For JBR, KIR and ABR.

Everything I do is for you guys.

HARLEQUIN
INTRIGUE

ISBN-13: 978-1-335-59111-1

Recycling programs
for this product may
not exist in your area.

Wyoming Cowboy Undercover

Copyright © 2023 by Juno Rushdan

For questions and comments about the quality of this book, please contact us at CustomerService@Harlequin.com.

Harlequin Enterprises ULC
22 Adelaide St. West, 41st Floor
Toronto, Ontario M5H 4E3, Canada
www.Harlequin.com

Printed in U.S.A.

Juno Rushdan is a veteran US Air Force intelligence officer and award-winning author. Her books are action-packed and fast-paced. Critics from *Kirkus Reviews* and *Library Journal* have called her work "heart-pounding James Bond-ian adventure" that "will captivate lovers of romantic thrillers." For a free book, visit her website: www.junorushdan.com.

Books by Juno Rushdan

Harlequin Intrigue

Cowboy State Lawmen

Wyoming Winter Rescue
Wyoming Christmas Stalker
Wyoming Mountain Hostage
Wyoming Mountain Murder
Wyoming Cowboy Undercover

Fugitive Heroes: Topaz Unit

Rogue Christmas Operation
Alaskan Christmas Escape
Disavowed in Wyoming
An Operative's Last Stand

A Hard Core Justice Thriller

Hostile Pursuit
Witness Security Breach
High-Priority Asset
Innocent Hostage
Unsuspecting Target

Tracing a Kidnapper

Visit the Author Profile page at Harlequin.com.

CAST OF CHARACTERS

Rocco Sharp—An ATF agent who must go undercover and infiltrate the Shining Light cult, but on this mission, he isn't prepared for what he discovers.

Mercy McCoy—The daughter of a cult leader. She may appear naive and fragile, but deep down, she's tough as nails and willing to fight for what she believes in.

Marshall McCoy—The charismatic leader of the Shining Light. He will do anything to safeguard his compound, his people and his secrets.

Nash Garner—FBI supervisory special agent leading the special joint task force investigating the Shining Light.

Charlie Sharp—Rocco's cousin and owner of the Underground Self-Defense school.

Brian Bradshaw—Laramie police detective assigned to the task force. Rocco's best friend and Charlie's boyfriend.

Chapter One

A gunshot fractured the quiet night.

ATF agent Rocco Sharp stiffened behind the wheel of his parked Ford Bronco, where he was waiting to meet his informant. Darkness wrapped around him on the overlook of the mountain, surrounded by trees. Which was the point. To pick a location where prying eyes wouldn't see them.

A cool August breeze washed over him through the rolled-down window. His skin prickled. He climbed out of the SUV and listened, hoping it wasn't another bad sign. The first had been that his contact was late.

In nine months, Dr. Percival Tiggs had never once been late.

Pop! Pop!

More gunfire ripped through the night. To the west. Far in the distance, but it sounded closer than the first shot. He reached into his vehicle, tapped open the glove box and grabbed the binoculars that were beside a flashlight. From this catbird seat, he had a view of the road below, as well as the mountainside and the river bathed in moonlight. He could easily see an approaching vehicle.

Peering through the binoculars, he focused all his attention on the twisting road that cut through the canyon and mountains. He picked up the soft purr of a finely tuned engine along with the rumble of low gears and the growl of a powerful V-6. Possibly V-8. Getting closer.

Sure enough, headlights pierced the darkness. A light-colored vehicle raced down the narrow, treacherous road. Rocco recognized the make and model. Old school. Vintage-style Land Cruiser.

Percival.

Was he blown?

Right behind him was a black heavy-duty hauler truck with two rear wheels on each side—a dually. Orange muzzle flashes burst in tandem with gunshots fired from the passenger's side of the truck at the sedan. Metal pinged. Sparks flared. The sedan zipped past the turn for the overlook.

Had Percival missed it deliberately to keep from leading anyone to Rocco? Or had he simply been going too fast to take the turn?

Either way, it wasn't good for Percival.

Before he lost sight of them, Rocco tried to home in on the rear bumper of the truck to get the license plate. He rotated the focusing ring on the binoculars, sharpening the image. There was a tinted film and splattered mud over the plate, making it impossible to read. But he glimpsed two bumper stickers. One with an iridescent silver tree on a white background. The other was red and scratched. A white bolt of lightning ran through it.

The vehicles disappeared around the curve of the road. Swearing to himself, he hopped in his Bronco and took off down the path that would converge with the road. They were a good thirty-minute drive from the outskirts of town, but still within the sheriff's jurisdiction. The special task force he worked on had a good relationship with the department. He called Dispatch and relayed the details of the truck in case they had a deputy in the vicinity who might be able to intercept. Wyoming Highway 130 crossed twenty-nine miles through the Medicine Bow Mountain Range. If they stayed on it, they'd be near Laramie.

"Headed east on WYO 130," he said, taking a hard right turn onto the road, kicking up dirt, "but they haven't passed Wayward Bluffs yet." That was the first town on the outskirts of the mountain range before Laramie.

"Agent Sharp, we don't have any deputies in the area," the dispatcher said. "But Deputy Russo was checking out a disturbance at the Wild Horse Ecosanctuary—"

"That'll have to do." He knew the location. About twelve miles from Wayward Bluffs.

Rocco clicked off the call and put the phone in his pocket.

No guarantees that Angela Russo would make it in time, but it was worth a try.

Red taillights came into view. Rocco pressed down on the accelerator, desperate to catch up. To give Percival a chance to lose whoever was chasing him. But with the winding road he could only risk going so fast.

A hairpin turn was coming up, but a thicket of tall pines would obstruct his view. Both vehicles took the acute bend. Through tree branches, he barely made out their lights.

Rocco slapped the steering wheel. Despite the air whipping over him, sweat rolled down his spine.

Recruiting an asset like Percy was a tricky game. Endangering the life of another. Trying to balance it with protecting them while pushing them to get the information needed. Someone was selling ghost guns—untraceable firearms—along with machine guns, military-grade explosive devices and specially marked armor-piercing bullets. Almost anything was legal in the Wild West of Wyoming, except the explosives, but the supplier was trafficking the deadly weapons and ammunition across state lines, putting them in the hands of criminals and gangs.

Innocent lives were being lost. Just last week, two fellow ATF agents out of the Denver office had been critically wounded in a raid. Armor-piercing rounds had punched through their Kevlar vests. Bullets from the same supplier that he'd been after for a year.

One of those agents had been a close friend. This was now personal for him. Still, he didn't want to jeopardize Percy's safety.

The ends didn't always justify the means.

Rocco whipped around the hairpin bend, his tires squealing against the asphalt. The scent of burned rubber stung his nose. On the straightaway, he could see them clearly headed downhill. He hit the accelerator harder, eating up the distance between them.

Pop!

The sedan's back windshield exploded.

Pop! Pop!

Percy's car swerved, fishtailing, like a tire had been blown out, and he lost control. The sedan went into a spin, crashing into the guardrail. Metal screamed. Brakes whined in the night. Sparks flew. With an agonizing shriek, steel sheared.

Rocco's gut clenched.

Lay off the brakes, Percy. Straighten out the wheel Come on.

The groan of metal rending filled the air as the ca broke through the guardrail. The sedan flipped over th side, bounced, and rolled toward the vast, deep maw o the ravine.

No. His stomach tightened even harder, his heart ham mering in shock.

The truck slowed a moment, passing the gaping hol in the guardrail and then raced off down the road.

Rocco jammed his foot on the gas until he reache the site of the crash. He noted the mile marker an threw the SUV in Park. Slapped the button for the haz ard lights. Snatched his flashlight. Tossed his cowbo hat on the seat. Dashed from the vehicle.

Adrenaline surged through him. He ran to the tor guardrail and shone the flashlight over the side. Th wrecked car was upside down. Nothing more than hunk of battered, twisted metal. A tree had stopped it descent toward the river.

Be alive, Percival.

Rocco jumped, catapulting down the hill. He lande hard and unevenly, turning his left ankle. A stabbin pain shot up his leg as he teetered off balance. H righted himself and hurried onward over the steer rocky terrain. Stumbled. Fell. Gasping, he was up o his feet. He was running at an angle down the slop now, trying not to slip again. His heart pumped fur ously. Sweat dripped from his brow.

One thought drove him. *Get to Percival.*

The man was a fifty-year-old veterinarian. Had a wife. A son. Had done nothing wrong besides having the right type of access at a time when Rocco's task force was in dire need of answers.

He slid down to the car. Shattered glass glittered in the moonlight. A bloody arm hung out the window.

Kneeling, he shone the flashlight up inside the car. The airbag had deflated. Blood covered Percival's face. Rocco pressed his fingers to the man's carotid artery, checking for a pulse. He found one. Thready. Barely there. But his informant was still breathing.

Rocco unsheathed his tactical blade from the holster clipped on his hip. He sliced the seat belt—the one thing that had saved Percival's life—and hauled him free of the wreckage over to a somewhat level spot.

Percival coughed. His head rocked side to side.

Rocco cradled the man's head in his lap, whipped out his phone from his pocket and dialed the sheriff's department once more. "Agent Sharp again. I need an ambulance." He relayed the mile marker. "The shooter got away in the black pickup truck still headed east on 80." Percival reached for him, mumbling something, but he couldn't hear what it was over the dispatcher's response. He glanced down. The injured man was clutching his abdomen. His shirt was soaked with blood. But he hadn't been impaled by anything in the car. Had he been shot? "There are at least two individuals in the truck. Hurry with that ambulance."

He dropped the phone, not bothering with hanging up, and pressed a palm to Percival's abdominal wound to slow the bleeding.

"He kn-kn-knew…" Percival coughed up blood. "
was a CI…" Another cough. More blood.

"Shush, don't talk. The ambulance is on the way.'
But at the rate he was bleeding out it wouldn't reach
him in time.

"No time," Percival said on a pained groan, echoing
Rocco's thought. *"Wrong."* With a trembling hand, he
dug in the pocket of his jeans and pulled out something
"We had it wrong."

Rocco took the balled-up wad and lowered it into the
light. The bloodstained paper had a date written on it
September 19.

Six days from now. "What happens on the nine
teenth?"

Percy shook his head. "Something big." His voice was
faint. "S-s-something horrible." His eyelids fluttered, his
breath growing shallow. He mumbled more words, too
low for Rocco to make out. "…planned it all."

"Who?" Rocco patted his cheek. Worry clawed a
him as he watched the life draining from this poor man
"What's going to happen? Who planned it?"

Percy's lips moved, but the whisper was lost in the
wind.

"Say it again." Rocco brought his ear closer to his face

"Mc-C-Coy. Ma…" The syllable slipped from Per
cival's mouth in his dying breath. His head lolled to the
side in Rocco's arms, his eyes frozen open at the mo
ment his life slipped away.

No! Rocco tightened his arms around Percy as if by
doing so he could change his fate. "God, no."

He thought of Percy's wife—his widow—and the rea
son for his senseless murder.

McCoy. Marshall McCoy.

Guilt seized his heart and squeezed. Followed by a wave of white-hot rage.

"I'll find out who did this to you," he vowed. He'd track down those men in the truck one way or another. And I'll make them pay."

Rocco knew precisely where to start.

With Mercy McCoy.

Chapter Two

Mercy McCoy padded through the entryway of polishe[d] steel and ten-foot-high windows that spanned the wall beneath a gleaming chandelier and across a veined ma[r]ble floor. At the door, she pulled on her canvas shoe[s] and stepped outside. She descended the steps of Lig[ht] House. It was her home, with private family quarte[rs] upstairs, but it also operated as the main building for t[he] entire commune. On the first floor, meals were preppe[d] and served where they ate together in the dining ha[ll.] This was the place where they gathered in celebratio[n] as well as mourning.

She slipped into the back seat of the SUV. She a[b]horred being chauffeured around and would've pr[e]ferred to sit up front, but her father had forbidden it.

As I am your father, I cannot also be your frien[d.] Not if I'm to do right by you. We are both leaders [of] the Light. You must know your place as everyone in t[he] flock must know theirs.

She gritted her teeth against the rule.

Alex, the head of security, pulled off from the c[ir]cular drive, taking the path downhill. "This is your la[st] time going into town for personal reasons."

Mercy swallowed around the cold lump in her throat. What? I don't understand. Why?"

"Empyrean's orders," he said, referring to her father, e great leader of the Shining Light.

"But he didn't say anything to me." She had seen him few minutes ago. He'd simply smiled and waved. Not word about any changes in protocol.

"I believe he wants to speak with you about it when)u return," Alex said.

Her chest tightened. "Is this a temporary thing? Or :rmanent?"

Alex met her questioning gaze in the rearview mir- ·r. He didn't respond, which was an answer in itself.

She scrubbed her palms down her thighs, her fingers ddenly aching. Mercy glanced over her shoulder back Light House. At the luminous glass-and-metal cage.

Whenever she left to go to town—for herself and not an acolyte bringing the word of their religious move- ent to others—she was usually filled with a pure joy at was as bright and warm as the sun. Mainly because had absolutely nothing to do with her father.

Tonight, nausea roiled through her. The wrought-iron ites of the compound opened. They drove through, issing the guardhouse. Towering trees obscured a ick wall that surrounded the property's one hundred res. She faced forward as they headed to town.

For six months, she'd had it good, able to leave the mpound twice a week. At first, it was for a hot yoga iss. Then she'd passed the Underground Self-Defense hool. She'd watched Charlie Sharp teaching a class other women. Showing them how to be strong, ca- ble. Fearless.

That was what she wanted to be.

Inside the compound, she was sheltered. Lived [in] a bubble of strict rules. The price of being afforded [a] constant sense of safety and peace. But always und[er] the umbrella of being Empyrean's daughter.

Out here, in the world, she often felt like a newbo[rn] foal running for the first time. Unsteady. Unsure. U[n]easy.

But when she was at USD, throwing punches a[nd] kicks, she was on fire. She was *free*. To discover hers[elf] and all the possibilities that existed beyond the walls [of] the compound. To see what she might be without t[he] Shining Light.

Now she was forced to do the one thing in the wo[rld] that she did *not* want to do.

Give it up.

Alex stopped on the corner of Garfield and Thi[rd] Street since he knew she didn't want anyone from U[SD] to see her being dropped off like a child.

She was twenty-four years old. But she didn't ha[ve] a license. Had never lived anywhere other than on t[he] compound. Never gone to a regular school. Never eat[en] a meal that hadn't been prepared by the hands of tho[se] she called family. Never been to a movie. Never ha[d a] job that paid money. Never had a Christmas tree. O[r a] birthday cake.

Never donned any color but white. Leaders we[ar] no hue, reflecting and scattering visible waveleng[ths] of light.

All per her father's edicts.

A restlessness bubbled inside her, spreading a[nd] seeping through every cell.

Her father meant well. She suspected his overprotec-
eness came from the loss of her mother when she was
young to remember her. He never talked about her,
d she'd learned not to ask questions to avoid causing
n pain. But the rules and restrictions everyone else
her community appreciated she now found stifling.

"I'll be back to pick you up at six forty-five." Alex
shed her a smile in the rearview mirror.

Her lungs squeezed. "That's okay. I'll walk back."

He turned in his seat and stared at her, his hazel eyes
ing to peel away her layers, see what she was hiding.
ex had learned that look from her father. He'd got-
very good at it. At twenty-nine, he'd been with the
ovement from the beginning, before she was born.
th each passing day he emulated the Empyrean more
d more. His title might be head of security, but he
s one of their top missionaries, guiding and coun-
ing, ever expanding his role. As much as he longed
someday take over as leader, she would never see
n as a shepherd.

Only as a big brother.

"Your father expects you home by seven," Alex said.
time for dinner."

She curled her fingers in fists, her nails biting into
palms, and nodded. As if she'd ever forget her fa-
r's schedule or his expectations. "I'll be there. On
e."

Alex glanced at his watch. "Then you won't be able
take the full class and walk back. You'll have to
ose."

Why did her choices always involve her sacrificing
nething?

"I'll drive you," Alex said, giving her another gr
that made her skin crawl. "Make it easy on you."

But she didn't want easy. To be kept in a gilded ca₉
being told what to do from sunrise to sunset.

Mercy swallowed the bile rising in her throat. "N
father gave no order that I had to be driven back. I
he?"

Alex's gaze fell. "No. He did not."

"Then I'll figure it out and make my own way bac
She was twenty minutes early for her class. If her train
Rocco, was already there, then she could have both.

No sacrifice required.

"This isn't the best time to be doing things on yc
own," Alex said.

"Why not?" It occurred to Mercy that the change
protocol might not be about her. "Did something ha
pen? Was a threat made against us?"

Not all the folks in town accepted the Shining Ligh
presence. A few were curious. Others feared them,
being different, for following a path that seemed o
She saw how people looked at her, dressed in all wh
The way they whispered as she passed.

On occasion, during the select new moons that E
pyrean dictated, they went to town en masse. Fi
strong, wearing T-shirts that advertised their messa
Handed out flyers at the bus station and other chos
spots in town, offering food and shelter for those
need. It wasn't uncommon for someone to throw a
mato or an egg at them. Sometimes even rocks.

She had never experienced any problems while
herself. Maybe it was the large group that was hard
ignore and easy to fear.

Once they had received a death threat at the com-
und. A terrifying time. But her father had put the
npound on lockdown and had beefed up security.
ne of which had happened today.

Mercy might've been questioning which path was
ht for her to follow because her father had never
en her a choice. Unlike everyone else in his flock.
t she believed in the callings. Witnessed how those
o came to them broken, in need, had found healing
l purpose. Regardless of what she ultimately decided
herself, she was willing to protect that sanctuary
those who wanted it, as well as her father's legacy.

"No, nothing like that. No threats," Alex said. "Em-
ean wants us to tighten our ranks. Focus more on
Light and less on the secular. He wants you to focus
re."

There it is.

This was about her. It was just as personal as she'd
pected. What irked Mercy more was that her father
l confided in Alex about *her* before speaking to her
iself.

Mercy never should've let it show how empowered
l happy she felt after a training session. Should've
den her feelings better. She'd been well-trained and
l let her guard falter.

You idiot. Stupid fool.

She'd brought this onto herself. It had always been
latter of time before Empyrean would take away
one thing that she had which was untouched by the
vement.

"I'm certain my father will discuss it with me later.

Thank you for the ride." Even though she didn't mea
it, there was no reason to be rude.

She got out and closed the door.

A passerby looked at her from head to toe, taking
her Shining Light pendant that dangled from her neck
a crescent moon with a sun—plain white T-shirt, matc
ing leggings and canvas shoes. The woman's mou
pressed into a thin line before she crossed the stre
like she didn't want to get too close to her.

Lowering her head, Mercy hurried down the stre
to USD, hating that this would be her last session. S
pushed through the front door and shoved aside t
creeping sensation of doom.

"My apologies for being late. It couldn't be helpe
said FBI Supervisory Special Agent Nash Garner, ta
ing a seat at the head of the conference room tab
where the rest of the team had been waiting for hi
"I'm sorry you lost your CI last night."

Nash oversaw the special task force. Their missi
was to investigate the Shining Light cult and dete
mine their threat level as possible domestic terroris
Throughout their investigation, an arms dealer ha
come onto their radar, one who was supplying the c
with their cache of weapons.

Rocco slapped his hand down on the evidence b
that contained the bloodstained piece of paper wit
date. "Percy died trying to tell me something. Wh
ever it is will happen in five days. I need permission
implement plan C." Alpha and Bravo had failed, lea
ing them with no other recourse.

Wary glances were exchanged around the room.

Special Agent Becca Hammond rested a hand on her
gnant stomach and rubbed what looked like a basket-
l under her shirt. She was only six months along and
eady all belly, but he'd never seen her more content
be working a desk instead of out in the field. "There
to be another way," she said.

It wasn't how he wanted to proceed either. Rushed.
phazardly. But now that a CI had been discovered—
rdered—his task force was out of time.

Figuratively and literally.

Taking a breath, Rocco glanced at his watch. Mercy
s at USD by now, waiting on him. To be early was
be on time for her. A trait he admired. He'd texted
cousin and asked Charlie not to let her leave. "They
led Percy because they're aware the authorities are
king into them. Any steps we take will be more dan-
ous now than ever before. The one informant you
l embedded in that cult went quiet because they got
red," Rocco said to Becca.

She lowered her gaze. Whoever her CI was—she had
er revealed their identity—had abruptly cut off com-
nication last month. Now with Percy gone they were
d in the water.

"We need to find that arms dealer," Rocco said. "The
ne one supplying the Shining Light. And we've only
five days to figure out whatever is supposed to hap-
and stop it." *Something important. Something hor-
le.* "Mercy McCoy is the key."

Brian Bradshaw, a detective with the LPD, leaned
ward. "Are you sure that's the only move?" The ques-
n coming from his best friend—who was also close

to becoming family as he was in a serious relationsh
with his cousin, Charlie—gave him a moment of paus

But only one. Rocco was aware that everyone at t
table was wondering the same thing. "I'm sure. Unle
someone else has a better idea."

Silence.

The only sound in the room came from Becca ope
ing a bag of pretzels. It was the only thing he'd se
her tolerate while she had morning sickness, which f
her, lasted all day and throughout the pregnancy so f;

He did not envy women.

"I need an answer. Now." He needed it ten minut
ago.

"How close is Mercy to being recruited as an asset
Becca asked. "I got the impression from your repo:
that she wasn't ready yet."

Her impression was spot-on. Mercy had shown sig
of discontentment with the movement, but that did
mean she'd be disloyal. Rocco didn't know if she wou
ever be prepared to spy on her father. "I want to a
proach it from a different angle. I already threw o
person into the fire and got them killed." The weig
of that rested heavy on his shoulders. He couldn't ev
give his condolences to Mrs. Tiggs and take respon
bility for what had happened because it would expo
his identity.

"It wasn't your fault that Percival was murdered
Nash said.

But the words rang hollow to Rocco. Sure, he had
been the one to pull the trigger. All the same, he'd ma
Percy a target.

"I won't endanger Mercy like that." She was you

1 kind. And beautiful. Had her whole life ahead of
. She hadn't asked to be born into a cult. But the day
'd walked into his cousin's school, asking about self-
ense classes, looking like a lost lamb, he'd seen a
den opportunity to cultivate the best asset. Over the
nths, he'd gotten to know her. First through group
ning sessions. Then later, one-on-one with him. He'd
wn quite fond of her. If he was being honest, it was
re than that. Every time they were alone together
vas getting harder to resist the fierce attraction be-
en them, but he forced himself to tamp the feeling
vn. Way down deep into oblivion. The last thing he
ld afford was any kind of attachment to a potential
et. "I don't know what her father would do to her if
found out."

Becca opened a bottle of water and took a sip. "From
at I know of Marshall McCoy based on his psych pro-
, he wouldn't kill his daughter." She was the resident
ert on the Shining Light.

"There are some punishments worse than death,"
cco said. "Are you positive that he wouldn't hurt
?"

"No." She shook her head. "'Through pain comes
ement. Only through the crucible can one find en-
tenment.' Those are a couple of their tenets. He'd
justified in hurting her if necessary."

Rocco clenched his jaw right along with his fist
ler the table. "Because of that and the fact that Bec-
right that Mercy isn't ready to turn on her father, I
nt to use her to gain access to the compound instead."

Becca choked on her water as the other two men
red at him in disbelief.

"You want to go undercover?" Nash asked. "Insi
the Shining Light?"

Rocco shrugged. "I do it all the time." It came wi
the territory of working for the Bureau of Alcohol, T
bacco, Firearms and Explosives. There was even a ter
for their elite undercover agents—Rat Snakes.

In the pioneer days, rat snakes were kept in jars a
unleashed to kill the enemy—eliminating rodents-
and then retrieved and put out of sight until the ne
infestation. The bureau used their covert operatives
the same way to rid the world of the worst criminals

Only those clever and strong enough got inside a
survived. Rocco was still standing. But he'd had to
things that most couldn't and wouldn't stomach.

"My cover is solid," Rocco said. Constantly chan
ing every time that he relocated for a new assignmen
this one he'd built around his cousin Charlie. T
best cover had elements of truth. So, he was using h
mother's maiden name, Sharp, and kept his military re
ord with some alterations that hinted at a walk on t
dark side. Threw in civilian gigs that wouldn't raise a
eyebrows, including a stint at a private security fir
that a friend of his owned up north. He'd made sure a
check run on him wouldn't break his cover.

"You've infiltrated every kind of scumbag group o
there from organized crime to notorious outlaw moto
cycle gangs," Brian said. "But not a cult."

"I thought tapping Mercy as an asset was the wor
idea," Becca said. "Until you suggested going inside t
compound." She shook her head, not liking the idea

"What if you two sat down with Mercy together"
Brian suggested. "Impressed upon her the urgency, th

es are on the line. Is it possible you two might be able
persuade her?"

"Possible," Becca said, hitching up a shoulder. "Not
bable. She doesn't see the Shining Light movement
a potential threat and may never. But I prefer the idea
talking to her, trying to work her as an informant,
tead of you jumping into the lion's den, Rocco."

The image of Percy's car going through the guardrail
ne back to him. His bloody face, his abdomen bleed-
, his life slipping away in Rocco's arms. All because
cco had pushed him to be an informant when he'd
rned Percy's son was part of the cult.

This was a cold, hard business that required them to
ke ruthless decisions in order to catch the bad guys.
t this was the first time he'd been rattled to the core.
Usually, his informants were criminals who'd been
erced. People who had already put their own lives
risk, and he was merely making it count for some-
ng good.

Percy had been an affable vet, healing animals and
ping them alive.

Mercy was even more innocent.

"And if you're wrong?" Rocco asked. "Then not only
e I lost an asset but also my one way inside the com-
und." He turned to Nash. This was the head honcho's
l to make and no one else's. "We have five days. I
n't want any more blood on my hands." And the one
he was willing to risk this time was his own. "Give
the green light on this."

If Nash didn't, Rocco would go forward with the
n anyway. Even if it meant he had to surrender his

badge when it was all said and done. Saving his care
didn't matter.

Only doing everything in his power to stop whatev
was in the works for the nineteenth.

"When's the next time you see Mercy?" Nash aske

"I'm supposed to be with her right now." They h
training sessions every Tuesday and Thursday. Th
was their last class for the week. The next time he sa
her would be too late.

"Do you really think you can convince her that y
want to join her father's religious movement after mont
of planting the seeds of all the things that might be am
with the Shining Light?" Nash asked.

There was no denying that it would be a gigan
stretch. Like leaping across the Grand Canyon.

"Maybe if you had a week, a couple of opportun
ties to warm her up to the idea," Becca said before
responded. "But out of the blue? Blindsiding her?" S
shook her head.

Frustration welled in Rocco's chest. Becca was us
ally the impulsive one, willing to take long-shot chanc
He thought he'd have her support on this. "We don't ha
a week," he snapped. "I don't even have two more mi
utes to spare discussing this. I need to leave."

Becca sighed. "Broach the subject tonight careful
You'll have to ease her into the idea. Their moveme
only accepts novices during the new moon. I don't thi
that's for a couple of weeks." She picked up her pho
and swiped through a screen. "One angle you mig
want to try is that by letting you into her communi
she would be helping you in some way on a person

el. One of their core beliefs centers around selflessly
ing those in need. That might work with her father."

The clock was ticking. He'd try anything.

Becca swore and looked up from her phone. "The
eteenth, this Tuesday, falls on a full moon...during
eclipse. I don't know what that means. If it's bet-
or worse. Everything that they do is based on the
ar cycle."

"What does a regular full moon mean for them?"
sh asked.

"It's a significant time for transformation." She
ugged. "I know more about the new moon when
vices who choose to stay are inducted. Marriages
blessed."

Playing this safe wasn't an option. "I've been the
e working Mercy's recruitment," Rocco said to Nash.
know her best. I think I can persuade her." His gut
d him to use the rapport he'd built—the natural con-
tion they had. "I just need a thumbs-up from you."

cking another impatient glance at his watch, he
nched his jaw and stood. "What do you say?"

Was this going to be a sanctioned op or was he going
gue?

Nash's stone-cold gaze slid to Becca for a second of
liberation coming back to him. "You're a go. Find
ir arms supplier and figure out what's planned for
nineteenth. You've only got one chance at this with
. Do whatever it takes."

Chapter Three

Anxiety wormed through Mercy. She paced around th[e] private training room, like a hamster on a wheel.

"Can I get you anything before my class starts?" Cha[r]lie asked, popping her head inside, yet again. "A bott[le] of water? A cup of tea?"

"No, thank you." Mercy chewed the inside of her bo[t]tom lip and fiddled with her pendant.

"Want to join us until he gets here?"

Mercy shook her head once. She'd started out wi[th] group classes, but that wasn't how she wanted to en[d] her last day.

"Okay. Sit tight." Charlie was lean and athletic. N[ot] one pushover bone in her body. A real spitfire.

Mercy admired her spunk and independence. Sh[e] would've traded every drop of her quiet resilience f[or] a glimmer of Charlie's fire.

"He's on his way," Charlie said, her smile soft, h[er] green eyes pleading. "I promise." She strutted awa[y] with that fearless air about her.

Mercy had already warmed up, stretched, and h[er] muscles were loose, raring to go. Still, no Rocco. Sh[e]

dn't know how much longer she'd be able to wait de-
ite the assurances that he'd be there.

The thought of not being able to see him and say
odbye gnawed at the pit of her stomach.

Maybe him not showing up was a sign that she should
bmit to her father's will. Be grateful for what she'd
en given. If not for his generosity in granting her such
eway to begin with and paying for her classes, she
ver would've enjoyed the luxury of training at USD.

Releasing a sharp sigh, Mercy turned, headed for
e door. But Rocco stepped across the threshold, en-
ring the room, his strides confident, strong, hurried.
His gaze locked on her, setting off an unmistakable
utter deep in her belly.

She suspected he had that effect on most women.

Tall and powerfully built. Skin the color of teak.
verything about him was strong and formidable like
e dense hardwood tree. He was handsome, too, in an
most painful way. The kind that stabbed her in the
est, reminding her that someone like him would never
 with someone like her.

Whenever she saw him, her palms would sweat as
o words sprang to mind…good *god*. Not as in an ac-
al deity. No man was a god. Not even her father, no
atter how hard he tried to ascend to such unreachable
ights. But Rocco was straight from the pages of an
d-world myth.

He took off his cowboy hat and speared his fingers
rough his longish brown hair. The strands fell to the
ckline of his snug T-shirt that did nothing to hide
e wide-shouldered, narrow-hipped rock-hard body
neath.

To think, she'd once been intimidated by him. T[
sheer size of him. The tribal tattoos running down o[
arm. The rough-and-tumble look. The scorching ma[
netism he exuded.

Then she'd seen how gentle and kind he was to all t[
women. After that she only wanted to train with hi[
One-on-one. In the private room.

A harried smile stretched across his kissable mout[
and she moistened her lips.

"Thanks for waiting, Mercy."

Even the way he said her name made her pulse lea[
Throat too tight to answer, all she could do was no[

"I know how precious and limited your time is her[
Rocco said.

He had no idea. But she shoved the thought from h[
mind, not wanting to dwell on it.

"It's okay," she muttered, finding her voice. "I'm ju[
glad you made it." She smiled. "I was afraid that you[
cancel."

"I hate missing a session with you. I look forwa[
to our hour together."

The feeling was mutual. "Me, too. The highlight of n[
week." The one thing in her life that had been all her[

"I didn't get a chance to change," he said, gesturi[
to his jeans before he dropped his duffel bag on t[
floor. "But I figured we could start with some spe[
drills. It'll sharpen your technique. Improve footwor[
Helps prepare you for real-world situations. Then we[
move on to slow sparring so you can work on seei[
the incoming movements. Retrain those panic reflex[
into functional ones, for proper evasive movements a[
counters."

Everything he'd said blurred together in her ears. [C]an we just jump to the slow sparring?"

"I know you want to get to the good stuff." He clasped [he]r shoulder, and a spark of something she couldn't name [u]nited within her—so intense, so raw that her body lit [up], every nerve ending coming alive with awareness. "[F]or some reason you seem to enjoy it when I fling you [to] the ground and pin you."

Pushing her to writhe beneath him until she executed [a c]ontortionist maneuver to break free.

Who wouldn't enjoy it?

Clearing her throat, she lowered her gaze. "I'm not [su]re I have time to do everything. I've got to be back [at] the compound by seven."

His grip on her shoulder tightened. Her pulse pounded [as] he leaned in close. He smelled sinfully good. The [y]ummy, woodsy scent of him had her thinking of the [mu]ltitude of rules she wanted to break.

"I can give you a lift," he said, low in her ear. "Drop [yo]u off close without anyone seeing. Like last time. Our [lit]tle secret." His smooth warm smile deepened.

Now all she could think about were the big, dirty [ki]nds of secrets she wanted to share with him. "Sounds [go]od." That would give her more time. With him.

He moved his hand, and her skin felt chilled.

She realized the hardest part of saying goodbye to [P]SD would be knowing there wouldn't be any more [m]oments such as these with Rocco.

He took off his shirt and stretched. Long, sinewy [m]uscles flexed across his back and abdomen. Her gaze [w]ent over the intricate lines of ink that wound over one [sh]oulder and inched across his sexy collarbone.

She swallowed hard, wondering what it would b
like to touch him. Not as a result of a self-defense mov
Purely for the sake of pleasure.

"Now that's settled," he said, "I trust you're ready fo
me."

In more ways than one.

Mercy had to suppress the thought, the urges tha
came over her whenever she was near him. She wa
only grateful her father didn't have a window into he
soul. He would be so disappointed.

"Yep." She hopped side to side on the balls of her fee
and stretched her arms. "I'm all warmed up."

Rocco put padded shin guards on her and then h
slipped on a pair of padded gloves. He held up his pro
tected palms and directed her through drills. A series o
rapid-fire punches, kicks and other strikes he'd taugh
her. She listened and responded with the appropriat
blows. They got into a quick, demanding rhythm. Bu
her heart was racing too hard. Too fast.

Working up a sweat, she struggled to suck in enoug
air. The room started to spin. Her pulse throbbed agains
her temples, her chest growing tighter and tighter. A
chill sliced through her. She stumbled back.

The strangest noise filled her ears—a sharp, keen
ing wheeze.

To her shock, the sound was coming from her.

"Mercy?" Rocco asked, worry coming over his face
"Are you okay?"

She nodded, but she couldn't breathe. Couldn't talk
Was she having a heart attack? Was she dying? "Am
bulance. I think I need an ambulance."

He ripped off the gloves and clasped her arms. She was shaking.

"Sit down." He guided her down to a mat. "Tell me what you're feeling."

She muttered off as much as she could through strained breaths.

"Close your eyes," he said, and she did. "Listen to the sound of my voice. I want you to inhale for a count of two. That's right. Exhale. One. Two." He repeated the instructions over and over, rubbing his warm hands up and down her arms until she was doing it. "Now I want you to inhale for a count of four." A pause. "Exhale the same. One. Two. Three. Four."

She didn't know how long it took, but eventually the shaking subsided and her lungs loosened.

"Open your eyes, Mercy."

When she did, he was crouched close in front of her. She met his gentle, concerned gaze. "I'm sorry."

"Don't you dare apologize."

She pressed a hand to her clammy forehead. "I don't know what happened."

"I think I do." He studied her face, frowning at whatever he saw there. "You had a panic attack. Have there been any big changes in your life? Anything different going on to cause you anxiety?"

Panic attack?

Sometimes her life behind the gates of the compound felt so small. Sometimes it was hard to breathe because her very existence was shrinking, withering, under her father's thumb. But this was the first time she had manifested any physical symptoms.

"This is my last training session." Dread bubbled

inside her, the thought of not having any future ses
sions with *him* unbearable. She warred with her sel
preservation instincts. "My father won't allow me t
come back."

"Why not?"

"It doesn't matter." Tears that she refused to she
pricked her eyes. She wasn't a spoiled brat. She neve
whined. Never complained. Only complied. Like a du
tiful daughter. "The point is I won't be able to see yo
anymore." She caught herself, at how that must hav
sounded to him. Embarrassment creeped through he
This was about Rocco more than anything else, but sh
didn't want him to know that. "I mean come back t
USD for training."

Rocco cupped her face in his big hand. Somethin
shifted between them, the air charging with latent elec
tricity. There was no denying her attraction to him
Every time she saw him it got harder and harder t
hide it.

But now she wondered if it was one-sided.

"Why do you stay with the movement?" He caresse
her cheek, sending tingles through her. "You don't seer
happy there."

Such a small question, but the answer was huge, lay
ered with years of habit and doctrine and love. Lov
for her community. Love for her father, as overbea
ing as he was.

The Light can illuminate. But it can also blind.

She dismissed that little voice in her head that crep
up in her moments of doubt. "It's complicated. I don
really have a choice."

He grimaced. "Are people forced to stay against their ill? I thought anyone could leave at any time."

Anyone but her. "The others aren't forced."

"But you are?"

She bit her lip. "It's getting late. There isn't time to plain it all to you."

"Then let me come with you to your community."

Reeling back, she stared at him in disbelief. "Into the mpound?"

"Yes."

"Why? To be reborn in the movement? I didn't think was for you." It was part of the reason she found him alluring, so appealing. He never judged and never nowed any interest in joining.

"I'm worried about you. So often you talk about your mily behind that wall, but not once have I ever heard ou mention any friends. It must be lonely."

He saw right through her. Was she that obvious to veryone? Or had she simply overshared with him?

"We could continue our training classes on the com- ound," he said. "Where I can watch over you. Be the iend you need."

Their time together had become a sort of therapy. She lked to Rocco in a way that she couldn't with anyone se. Asked him any question. No subject off-limits. o topic inappropriate. No fear of him reporting back hat was discussed.

She had an affinity with him that she wasn't ready lose.

Her mind whirled toward a black void. Bringing peo- e inside on a whim didn't happen. That wasn't how ings were done. Not how the Shining Light operated.

But she wanted a solution that didn't involve yet another sacrifice on her part. "I don't see how that's possible."

He took her hands in his. Her fingers instinctively clung to him, afraid to let go. To lose *this* forever. A chance at something different. A tether to the outside.

"You once told me that through the Light all things were possible. Do you remember?" he asked.

Of course she did. "I'm surprised you do."

"I listen to everything you say, Mercy." As his gaze slid over her, she sensed that he not only cataloged her every word, but also observed her every reaction. "You are Empyrean's daughter. You don't realize the power you have."

Power? She almost laughed at the absurdity of such a thing. Her father didn't even want her to succeed him when the time came for him to choose their next shepherd. He'd told her that she was unfit to assume the position.

She shook her head, wishing she could explain it to him, but ultimately, she was too ashamed.

"How many Starlights are in your commune?"

That was the new surname acolytes took once they were reborn in the sacred ceremony, shedding their former selves. Then they chose a new forename as well and were anointed with a tattoo of the Shining Light. The same design as her pendant, but on the tattoo in the center of the sun was an eye.

"Five hundred and twelve," she said.

"How many of them get to come to town twice a week to take classes?"

None.

"I'm betting it's only you. Because you have your

father's ear." Rocco squeezed her fingers, his gaze boring into her. "Why do you wear white?"

The question was rhetorical. She had explained the color system to him. At the Shining Light everyone had a function and wore a color that represented it. Security donned gray. Essential workers, green. The creatives—artists, musicians—wore orange. Yellow was reserved for counselors and educators. New recruits, novices considering whether to join were denoted by the color blue. "No hue for leaders," she said.

"Be a leader. Usher me into the Light. Where all things are possible."

His crazy logic made complete sense.

"The council of elders will question it," she said. "They can make things difficult." Unless her father condoned it, which wasn't likely.

Rocco shrugged. "Do any of them wear white?"

A calmness settled over her. "No." Her father had given the council a voice. But that was all. The elders could be loud and irritating, but they had no power. "But there's still my father to deal with. You don't know how he can be."

Unyielding.

Harsh.

The mountain that could not be moved.

"I don't want anything to happen to you." He searched her face for something. "Would he punish you? Beat you if you brought me inside?"

For this type of infraction? "No, but he'll fight me on it."

"Fight back. I've knocked you down countless times. And you always get up swinging. I've never seen you surrender. Not only are you strong, but you're a smart fighter. You think quickly on your feet. All you need to do is decide what you want. Then set your mind to it."

For months, he seemed to be luring her away from the Shining Light, daring her to question the teachings, tempting her to dream of a different life. Now he was inverting everything. A total flip. "Why would you do this for me? Put your life on hold to live among us?"

He looked at her with pity.

I am not fragile, on the verge of falling to pieces, she wanted to tell him. "I don't need you to save me." Mercy already had one man in her life dead set on doing that already. She didn't need another.

His features grew pained. He stroked his thumb over her cheek. The gesture was so tender and sweet, a tear rolled from her eye. Before she could whisk it away, he did it for her.

"It wouldn't be entirely selfless. I've been going through a rough time lately. Caught up with the wrong crowd. People who entice me to revert to unhealthy habits."

"Do you mean with drugs or alcohol?"

"Your questions are always so direct."

That was the way her father had raised her. Emotional transparency. Complete honesty. "I'm sorry."

"It's not an easy thing to talk about. But I need a break without the temptation. You'd be helping me out in a big way by sharing your community with me."

The principle of giving help when asked for was branded on her soul.

At the compound, the counselors were good at assisting people through rough patches. In their treatment essions, they would get him to talk about everything. Unburdening was an essential part of the process. "You might find the movement difficult to accept."

"I want to understand it. Your world. Your way of life on the compound. I want to see why so many choose to stay. Why you stay." His warm brown gaze fixed on her face. His expression was sympathetic. "Give me time to get to know you better. And you me." His voice was soft and comforting. "What do you want, Mercy?"

Change.

To have things on her terms for once. To step out of Empyrean's shadow.

Defiance prickled across her skin. She wanted to keep something for herself that her father held no dominion over. And this man she'd come to know and bonded with would not fall to his knees in blind worship of the Shining Light.

At least, she hoped not. Her father could be mighty persuasive.

But Rocco was tough and would not be easily swayed.

Embracing the rebellious idea, she tilted her head to one side, watching him as he did her, studying his ruggedly beautiful face. He was younger than he appeared. It was the threads of silver in his neatly trimmed goatee and around the edges of his hairline that made him look older than thirty-two. She remembered everything he told her also.

He stared at her with an intensity that left her trembling, but strength seeped through her as determination to take a chance set in.

Although Rocco only offered friendship, which was no small thing, to have a steady shoulder that was all hers to lean on—something she'd never had—she knew exactly what she wanted, even if it was only for a little while because he would never choose the Light.

And she could never truly leave it.

She wanted more moments with him. Private and special and hers alone.

She wanted Rocco.

Chapter Four

preparation for dinner, Marshall McCoy changed
om his white suit and button-down shirt into a simple
nite tunic with matching linen slacks. As he strode
refoot down the front staircase of Light House, a ve-
cle he didn't recognize pulled up the circular drive.

A Ford Bronco.

They didn't use that make and model at the comune.

Even more surprising, Mercy alighted from the pas-
nger's side. He continued down the staircase, staring
rough the floor-to-ceiling windows to catch a glimpse
the driver. Wearing a cowboy hat, the man strode
ound the front of the vehicle into the amber light.
arshall stopped, frozen in curiosity as to who he was.
e guy stood a head taller than the security guards
thering out front, or even Alex. His shoulders were
oader than average. Dark hair fell, brushing his col-
r and obscuring his face.

The armed guards parted for him like the Red Sea
Moses.

Whoever this cowboy was, one thing was certain.
was trouble with a capital T.

Quietly, Marshall watched them enter the house from his position on the staircase. Mercy guided the stranger to remove his shoes, putting her hand on his arm as she whispered something to him. The man had interesting features. His body looked as if it had been sculpted from stone, every muscle defined. Striking tattoos ran down his arm.

His little girl was now a grown woman. Although she had never shown the slightest romantic interest in anyone at the commune, Marshall could see what she might find appealing about this one.

In five seconds, he could tell the attraction was mutual. This man stood close to her. Closer than any of their guards had ever dared. They kept sharing little glances as if their gazes were drawn back to one another.

Marshall had to resist the urge to crack his knuckles.

Alex hung back behind them, looking uncertain. As though he was the interloper.

A sense of trepidation whispered through Marshall. The stranger did not belong here and yet he stood as if ready to conquer the compound.

"My daughter returns with a stranger." The warmth in his voice surprised even him. Extending his arms in welcome, he glided down the rest of the steps. "Who have you brought to us, my child?"

"Father, this is Rocco Sharp. He's my instructor at the Underground Self-Defense school. Rocco, this is Empyrean."

"The man my daughter has been grappling and getting sweaty with for six long months."

There was a deep, ugly silence like a festering wound. Mercy's cheeks flushed. Alex lowered his head.

But Rocco flashed pearly whites in a wide grin, moved his worn cowboy hat and proffered a hand. eased to meet you, sir." Not an ounce of shame. No h to dismiss the suggestive insinuation.

Gutsy.

"Forgive me for not shaking," Marshall said, pulling his stock smile that telegraphed grace. "I prefer to d a person's energy when they first enter my home." raised both palms. "May I?"

Without glancing at Mercy with uncertainty, he pped forward. "Certainly."

This was a strong one, not only of body, but also of rit. He would not be easy to break.

But would he be willing to bend?

Marshall took Rocco's head between his hands, ought his brow down to touch his, and then put a nd over his heart. Rocco didn't shutter his eyes as y looked at one another. This might have been a ring competition for the younger man, but Marshall s on a mission.

Closing his eyes, he breathed deeply, opening him- lf to the energy within this other soul. Letting it flow rough him.

There was darkness in him, as well as a powerful ght. A blaze burning inside Rocco. An unmistakable nse of violence. Yet also control. But his heart, beat- g powerful and steady as a metronome, was out of ach. Guarded.

This man was not lost. But he was searching. For mething.

As many who came here were.

Dropping his hands, Marshall said, "Come and let us

speak." Bringing his daughter to his side, he led the deeper into Light House, down the hall. He glanced Rocco as they passed the mural of the Shining Ligh symbol on the wall. The cowboy's eyes were draw to it, as were all newcomers. They reached his offic "Thank you, Alex," he said once inside. "Could yo wait in the hall and close the door?"

A flustered look came over his face, but Alex bowe his head. "Yes, Empyrean."

Marshall stood in front of his desk and clasped hi hands. "What brings you here to us, Rocco?"

"I brought him," Mercy said, quickly, "because—

Marshall held up a finger, silencing her. "I will g to you in a moment, my dear," he said while keepin his gaze focused on the stranger, his voice soft. "Rocc please answer for yourself."

"We've become friends. After she told me tonigh would be her last training session and that she didn know whether we'd see each other again, I asked if could come here. I've been going through a difficu time. Struggling with some things. I thought it migh be healthy to get away from negative influences. Com here to better understand your ways. And Mercy. She' always talking about her faith."

"You've had six months to satisfy your curiosity. Marshall stepped closer to him. "Why all of a sudden?

"I took for granted that we'd have more time togethe The idea of not seeing her again and going back to som dark habits made this feel urgent, sir. Like this was m chance, and I shouldn't blow it."

Marshall didn't detect a lie, but he also wasn't gettin the whole truth. "We only accept novices during cer

in new moons. If your interest remains in six weeks'
me, you may return to see if our beliefs and lifestyle
ould suit you. Thank you for bringing Mercy home."
e gestured toward the door.

"You misunderstand, Father. I've brought him here
s my *guest*," Mercy said. "Not as a potential novice."

Another whisper of unease—a faint sixth sense of
arning that this cowboy would be more than he could
ontrol.

This Rocco had already gotten his daughter to ignore
ustom and flout his basic edicts. What would be next?

To his credit, and as a result of five decades of faking
, Marshall didn't show the slightest hint of surprise or
nger, even though both were brewing inside him. He
ghtened his smile. "You know the rules, sweetheart,"
e said gently. "We do not bring in guests."

"We haven't, in the past," she said. "Exceptions can
ways be made."

"If I allowed this with you, every member of the flock
ight seek to do the same. We can't have anarchy, with
ur gates open wide."

The flash of disappointment in her eyes was undeni-
ble. As was the glimmer of determination. "You allow
xceptions with me whenever you see fit because I'm
ot like the rest of the flock. I'm a McCoy. Not a *Star-
ght*," she said. A powerful distinction. "He asked for
y help, and I was called to bring him here. That inner
oice you commanded me never to ignore spoke. I have
stened. You can't ask me to turn him away."

Was it the voice of a higher power?

Or that of Rocco's, flowing from poisoned lips into
er ear?

"I will reconsider our current timeline," Marsh▮ said, his voice light, his tone easygoing. "Instead of wa▮ ing six weeks, we will open our gates to potential n▮ ices, *guests*, at the next new moon." That should appea▮ her. What was she thinking, bringing a stranger here ▮ close to the full moon eclipse? Particularly this strang▮

Her blue eyes gleamed with a spark of rebellion th▮ threatened to set him off, but he kept his facade affab▮ "You don't care about my calling, do you?" she aske▮ "Or that I'm trying to help someone in need. I have ▮ place here. Not in the flock. Not as a leader. I'm not▮ ing more than a shiny fixture on your shelf."

The tighter he clung to her, the more determined s▮ seemed to slip free from his grasp. With each passi▮ year, the restlessness in her continued to grow to t▮ point where he could no longer ignore it. At first, ▮ had tried to pacify her by letting her run their qua▮ terly farmers' market. Then he put her in charge of t▮ novices.

Still, it wasn't enough.

The glint for more never left her eyes. So, when s▮ asked to take classes at USD, he'd thought, *what cou▮ be the harm?*

But those classes only poured gasoline on the burr▮ ing embers of doubt kindling inside her.

"We'll discuss this privately." Marshall would fin▮ some way to get her to see reason once she was outsid▮ this man's sphere of influence. He was going to be th▮ only one to pull his daughter's strings. Marshall turne▮ to the cowboy. "Excuse us."

Rocco cast a questioning glance at Mercy, waitin▮ for *her* to give him the okay.

His gaze slid back to his daughter. "Have your friend it in the hall or I will have security escort him there."

Straightening, Mercy shook her head. "No, you won't."

Laughter devoid of humor rolled from his chest. hile he found her refusal to back down, and pointly so, surprising, he didn't find it the least bit funny. ive me one good reason why not."

"Because I need something to change. We're too inlated and I'm suffocating." She clasped her hands hind her back, her chin jutting up, making her look ery bit the warrior that he had forged, though he never pected her to turn on him. "For seven years, you've nied me the right of *penumbroyage*. If you don't let m stay as a guest where he can learn about the Light d our ways, I'll claim it before the elders tonight. And ave with him to do what I can to help him out there yond the walls of the compound."

Her sharp sword cut deeply.

Marshall clenched his jaw against the bitter taste that ooded his mouth. When she was a teenager, she had own proficient at guerilla warfare with him, but he d learned to defend against her tactics. It was so rare r Mercy to stand up to him in a full-frontal attack like is that it completely blindsided him.

Turning, he strode to a window and stared out at e darkness.

"What is that? *Penumbroyage?*" Rocco asked.

Mercy looked at him. "Have you heard of rumringa?"

"It's like a rite of passage for Amish teens, where ey get to leave their community, live on the outside r a while before deciding to commit to their religion."

"*Penumbroyage* is the same for us," she said. "If y were born here or came in as a child, you can take year away between the ages of seventeen and twent four. My father has insisted that I've been needed he to help him. He keeps demanding that I delay it."

A request. Not a demand.

As Empyrean he couldn't strip her of the right th he himself created to safeguard the purity of the hear in his flock. He had stressed to Mercy the importan of her staying as a demonstration of faith. How wou it look to their community for her to have doubts abo their way? How poorly it would reflect on him as the shepherd if his blood needed distance to see the rig path to follow. The stain it would leave, tarnishing h legacy.

Aside from appearances and the shame that wou follow if she chose the secular world, he feared far mo than a blow to his ego. He would do anything to avo losing his only daughter.

Absolutely anything.

He never imagined that she would ever claim th right, taking a year away. With no money, no job, n place to stay, most didn't. The few young people wh did leave had family on the outside that they could tur to.

Part of Mercy had agreed to delay her sojourn be cause she was a good, devoted child. But the other par of her simply had nobody on the outside to rely on fo assistance.

Until now.

He stared at Rocco's reflection in the windowpane Watched him put a comforting hand to the small of he

ck. Witnessed his daughter's response. The sharp in-
e of breath, the flush to her cheeks, the way she looked
him. He saw every unnerving, nauseating detail.

The sexual tension between them was nuclear.

Marshall spun on his heel, facing them. "Have you
n with this man?" he asked, pouring all his concern
her than reproach into his voice.

Is that what was really going on during her one-on-
e sessions?

"Wh-what?" she stuttered, the color in her cheeks
epening.

The cowboy didn't flinch. Didn't even bat a lash.

"No." Mercy crossed the space separating them. "Fa-
er, I swear it. Not that it would be any of your busi-
ss if I had. You conveniently didn't make any rules
out chastity."

Rocco arched an eyebrow and gave a pleased-looking
od, which Marshall also caught. Maybe it was time he
ade such a rule.

He didn't want his people acting like free-loving
ppies with no sense of self-control or decorum. Still,
didn't preach celibacy. Only celebrated monogamy.
e permitted unions, often arranging them himself,
rmed matches and blessed marriages. Seldom was he
ithout a carefully picked partner himself. Currently
e was sleeping with the nubile Sophia, who worked
the garden, and things had become serious between
em despite his daughter's reservations.

"You were raised to treat your body as a temple."
Marshall cupped her arms. "Not to violate my trust by
ullying yourself with someone who is unworthy be-
ause he has not accepted the Light."

She narrowed her eyes. "I've done no such thing promise you."

Exhaling a soft breath of relief, Marshall force smile. "I needed to be sure of the purity of your inte tion in bringing him here." He had no choice but to ta her word for it. Even if she was telling the truth, h attraction to him, her desire to lie with him was ob ous. "I love you," he said, hugging her, "and only wa the best for you." Which didn't include her new frier

This man, who wrestled between the darkness a the light, would take her from him as surely as t sun rose in the east and set in the west. Unless he p a stop to it.

"I know you do," she said, pulling away and ste ping back.

"You are welcome here," he said to Rocco. "To sta To learn. To grow in the Light."

The corner of Rocco's mouth inched up in a grin ju shy of cocky. Marshall wanted to slap it off his face.

"Thank you, sir."

"You'll need to hand over your cell phone," Marsha said. "Most here are not allowed to have them, not ev Mercy. It is a distraction from growth."

"Your daughter told me. I left mine in the car. Alor with the keys."

"Good." Marshall nodded and turned back to h daughter. "Mercy, I will only ask one small thing in r turn for my generosity."

She stiffened. "What is it?"

"We'll discuss it at dinner." If he could not get he alone, then he would continue this discussion in from of the entire flock where she would not dare cause

ne. "Why don't you go get cleaned up and changed?
show Rocco into the dining hall and introduce him
he community, where we'll wait for you."

"Thank you." She rose on the balls of her feet and
sed his cheek. On her way out, she grazed Rocco's
n and gave him a reassuring smile.

The sweetness of it sickened him.

Marshall needed to act quickly. "Would you like to
sh up before dinner?" he asked Rocco.

"Yes, thank you."

"We passed the restroom in the hall. It'll be the first
your left."

With a nod, he exited the office. Once Rocco was
t of earshot, Marshall snapped his fingers and beck-
ed Alex.

His right-hand man, his son though not of his blood
t by choice, hustled into the room.

"I want you to run a background check on him,"
arshall said.

"I already did after it looked like Mercy would be
king classes at USD regularly."

Marshall motioned for him to continue. "And? What
d you find out? Criminal background? Deadbeat
d looking to duck out on making child support pay-
ents?" *Give me something to work with.*

They had all sorts show up seeking *refuge*. Even a
uple of fugitives from the law. All could be put to
od use in some capacity while he worked on healing
eir souls and mending their hearts.

Alex took out his cell phone, one of the few per-
itted inside the compound, and scrolled through the
reens. "Charlotte Sharp has owned the place for about

three years. She's his cousin. Goes by Charlie. The
grew up together. His mother is her aunt, and his pa
ents became her legal guardians. Rocco moved her
last year and started working at USD."

"What was he doing before that?"

"Military for a few years." Alex swiped through t
another screen. "His record was sealed."

"What does that mean?"

"He probably did special ops for them. But he di
get a dishonorable discharge. I couldn't find out wha
for. He floated around for a bit, worked as a bouncer
bartender and for a private security company befor
settling here as a self-defense instructor. No crimina
record. No marriages. No kids. But a couple of DUIs.

Clean. Except for that dishonorable discharge and
the DUIs. "You mentioned that Charlie is his mater
nal cousin?"

"Yes."

Then why did he go by Sharp if his parents were to
gether? "What's his father's name?"

Alex glanced back at his phone. "Joseph Kekoa."

"What kind of surname is that?"

"Hawaiian. I looked it up. It means warrior," Alex
said, sounding impressed.

"Do a search on Rocco Kekoa. See if anything comes
up. I need it fast."

"Will do," Alex said, making a note. "What's the
rush?"

"I've agreed to let him stay here with us for a while."

Alex paled. "But why?"

"Listen to me." Marshall put a hand on his shoulder
"The only thing you need to know is that tonight I'm

ing to give you the opportunity you've long waited
r. The one thing standing in your way is that cowboy.
n going to give him enough rope to hang himself and
ou're going to help me do it."

At the sound of approaching footsteps, Marshall
hooled his features.

Rocco waltzed back into the office. "My ears were
urning. Was I the topic of discussion?"

"As a matter of fact, you were." Marshall headed out
the office, gesturing for Rocco to walk with him. "We
ere trying to decide what work detail might best suit
ou while you're here. Do you know anything about
orses or farming?"

They headed toward the dining hall down the cor-
dor lined with art made by his followers.

"I grew up on a ranch. Love horses. But I've got
ome military experience. I'm better with every weapon
nder the sun than I am with animals. Or plants."

"Is that so?" Marshall nodded. "What did you do in
e military?"

"I'd tell you, but then I'd have to kill you." Rocco
ashed a smile that probably made women swoon and
udged him with his elbow like they were pals.

"Why not put him on security under me?" Alex said,
ollowing them closely. "I could show him the ropes."

Translation: keep an eye on him.

"I like the idea." Marshall gave a nod of approval.
But let's hold off on assigning him a firearm just yet."

"What are your reservations?" Rocco asked. "I as-
ure you I know how to handle myself and a weapon."

"I have no doubt about that," Marshall said, stopping

at the entrance of the dining room. "But I see you f
precisely what you are."

"And what is that, sir?"

"You're an agent."

Chapter Five

Rocco's heart skipped a beat, but he didn't let it show, keeping his features relaxed, his eye contact steady. "Come again?"

"You're an agent of chaos, Mr. Sharp. Sent to test me and the faith of my family. But my house is not built on sand and will weather any storm." Smiling, he put a hand on Rocco's shoulder and ushered him forward.

They entered a massive open space, large enough to be a ballroom, filled with wooden tables and chairs.

The dining hall was packed with a rainbow of Starlights. Green, gray, orange, yellow and blue sprinkled throughout the room. Everyone was seated. Plates filled with food in front of them, but no one was eating. From what he could see, no one wore shoes either. Mercy had explained that it wasn't allowed due to cleanliness.

A tense silence fell as all eyes turned to focus on them.

"My dear family," Marshall said, his voice bouncing off the walls of the hushed hall, "I want for you all to welcome Rocco. He will be our guest. Brought to us by your sister Mercy."

Murmurs flowed through the room like a current of air.

"I know this is unusual," Marshall said. "But yo[u] sister was called to help this man. We must support [her] as she blooms as a leader in answering what the Lig[ht] has asked her to do. I trust I can count on you. W[hat] say you all?"

In unison the group bowed their heads and said, "[So] shall it be."

Marshall glanced at Rocco. "Let's get some food," [he] said, indicating a long table set against the wall.

There were large aluminum tins of rice, rolls, [an] array of vegetables, beans and lentils. But no me[at.] "Looks like you all are vegetarians," he said, preten[d]ing to be surprised since he'd never discussed it wi[th] Mercy and didn't want to appear to know too much. [He] took a tray and put food on his plate.

"We believe in sustainable living," Alex said. "W[e] grow all our own produce. A plant-based diet lowe[rs] greenhouse gas emissions, reduces environmental de[g]radation and promotes a healthy lifestyle. We strive [to] make the world better."

That was quite a mouthful. "Well, this looks del[i]cious." Rocco was going to need a juicy double burge[r] once he got out of there.

"You should try a piece of pie," Marshall said, ge[t]ting a slice for himself. "There's strawberry rhubar[b] and pear. Baked fresh today by caring hands."

Rocco wouldn't turn his nose up at pie and went fo[r] the strawberry rhubarb.

They grabbed forks, cups of water, and proceede[d] to a table that had a few guys from the security tea[m] already there.

A young, attractive woman dressed in green made
eline for them, juggling a dinner tray.

With a shake of his head and subtle wave of his hand,
rshall said, "It would be best if you sat with the oth-
tonight, Sophia."

She faltered in her tracks, a disappointed look fall-
across her face. "Of course, Empyrean."

"But I would like to chat with you privately later in
quarters."

A huge smile broke out on Sophia's angular face. "I
k forward to our discussion." She turned and walked
ck to the table where she had been previously.

Marshall took a chair at the head of the table, made
roductions, and launched into a spiel. "Many get
red in the muck of the world beyond our gates, but
: are excellent at helping all unburden themselves.
u should be aware that you'll be expected to follow
r rules. Transgressions are frowned upon."

But Rocco's focus drifted when Mercy walked into
e dining hall.

A white cotton dress clung to slender curves, cupping
easts that were the perfect size for a lover's hands.
nny blond hair, no longer up in a bun, hung past her
oulders in long waves, framing a face that was too
gelic. Too pretty. She had an ethereal beauty. Radi-
ed light.

She was… Wow.

Her eyes—a fierce electric blue that rivaled the color
a summer sky—found his for a moment that didn't
st nearly long enough before she looked away.

She stopped at a table filled with children and briefly
id something that made them giggle. Others rose,

who'd been seated nearby, and flocked to her. Th
congregated around Mercy, speaking hurriedly as th
touched her shoulder or arm with warm, sympathe
smiles. They all seemed captivated by her, which w
no surprise to Rocco.

Finally given a break, Mercy approached their ta
with a plate of food. Rocco stood, shifting his pl
down one seat, and pulled out the chair for her next
her father.

"Thank you," she said and then lowered her voi
so only he could hear. "But please don't do that agair

He followed her gaze around the room. Everyo
was staring at them.

Was being a gentleman frowned on, too?

After she sat, Marshall raised his palms.

As a collective, they said, "Thank you for the gi
of this meal to sustain us. May it nourish our bodi
and fuel our ability to make this a better world, so w
may grow in the Light. We are grateful to embrace th
movement in the pursuit of truth."

Once their prayer was done, the community bega
eating and conversations resumed.

Marshall stood. "I have a glorious announcemen
One I have long hoped to make. The Light has finall
spoken to me on the matter, and the time has come fc
Mercy and Alex to open their hearts to one another an
begin a courtship."

Mercy's expression fell, like a building razed to th
ground by an implosion. She stared at her father, jav
unhinged, and then looked at Alex, who gave her ;
smile that was quite charming. If one was partial to rats

Based on her grimace, she wasn't.

This was the one *small* thing her father wanted in return for allowing Rocco to stay. He had to bite his tongue against a sudden surge of fury. He hated that was being used as a tool to coerce her.

"This is not my will," Marshall said. "But that of the light. What say you, Alex?"

The rat's grin spread wider, his eyes glittering. "So all it be."

"What say you, Mercy?" When she hesitated, her her added, "We do not get to pick and choose. All is ne for the greater good. What say you?"

Somehow Mercy appeared furious and torn at the ne time. Straightening her shoulders, she glanced ound the dining hall, at all the members of her comune waiting for her answer. The tension in the room as thick as smog, but far more toxic.

The tight hold this community had on her was evint.

"So shall it be," she said, lowering her head.

Raucous applause broke out in the hall along with eers.

Marshall sat and clamped a hand on her forearm. Have faith in the process. Many happy, successful nions have been made this way."

"You mean by forcing people together," Rocco said.

Marshall pulled on a pleasant expression that looked acticed. "In the US, the divorce rate is 50 percent. While over half the marriages worldwide are arranged nd have a divorce rate of only four percent. In thirty ears, out of all the unions I've put together, ninety-nine ercent have thrived."

Regardless of his statistics, her father neglected to

mention that sometimes "arranged" was merely a ve
neer, hiding abuse in the name of tradition. Oftentime
in developing countries access to divorce was limite
and many women found themselves trapped.

The truth behind the impressive percentages didn
discourage Marshall from giving his daughter a gentl
smile. "Sometimes the heart requires a nudge of en
couragement to open to the right person. It's easy to
be tempted by the devil." He threw a furtive glance a
Rocco. "But we are stewards of a higher power."

"Yes," she said, nodding. "I understand."

A litany of questions flew through Rocco's mind
about how this courtship process worked and whethe
it implied there'd be an engagement, but he'd have to
wait until he could speak with Mercy alone. Not that she
was anything more to him than an asset. Still, no one
deserved to be ramrodded into dating someone, much
less marrying them, especially if it was with slimy-
looking Alex.

"After dinner, Rocco," Marshall said, "Shawn will
take you to one of the bunkhouses for novices to get
you settled in." He gestured to a security guard at the
table he'd been introduced to earlier.

Mercy stiffened. "I'd like to show him around the
compound and take him over."

"You'll be busy after supper, sweetheart." Marshall
patted her arm again. "Spending time alone with Alex.
You have to make an effort for it to work."

She pinched her lips while Alex beamed like a kid
who was about to be unsupervised in a candy shop.

Gritting his teeth, Rocco wanted to hold her hand,
give her the slightest touch of reassurance, but there

ere far too many eyes on them. "I promised to con-
nue Mercy's self-defense classes. It's the least I can
. We should squeeze in one a day starting tomorrow."

Mercy perked in her seat, her eyes growing bright.
That's a great idea."

"I never really got why you needed those classes to
egin with," Alex said. "I taught you how to shoot." He
lared at Rocco. "You know, I'm a deadeye. No better
hot here than me. Bet I can teach her how to throw a
unch and a kick just fine."

Rocco cleared his throat to hide his chuckle. "There's
lot more to it than that. I'm trained in jujitsu and Krav
Maga. I'm teaching her how to survive and to handle
erself in close-range combat. Not a backwoods brawl."

Anger flashed over Alex's face as he clenched a fist.

Rubbing everyone the wrong way, regardless of
vhether he was provoked, wasn't going to do Rocco
iny good. He needed to make friends, but was well
on his way to only making enemies. "I'd be happy to
each you a few things," he said to Alex, trying to clean
up the mess he'd made. "And anyone else interested in
learning."

"We'll see if there's time," Marshall said. "You're
going to have full days, Rocco, starting at sunrise.
Morning meditation. Our daily gathering, where I and
others deliver homilies to the community. You'll need
to get acquainted with the security team. And of course,
there's the most important part, your unburdening session."

Alex glared at Rocco, but the others at the table nodded and chimed in, including Mercy, as though it were
vital.

Unburdening was their version of a *share-fest* wit
one of their counselors, where you talked about you
woes that brought you to the Shining Light.

He'd have to fake his way through it, which shouldn
be too hard. His life was full of wounds and emotiona
shrapnel that had taken him to dark places. Not that h
wanted any cult disciples digging around in his head. I
would be far better if he could figure out how to stav
off any unburdening altogether.

Whatever he did, he had to work quickly.

Two days.

Almost.

Rocco had been on the compound for forty hours
almost two days, and had discovered nothing.

He spun in mind-numbing circles to the beat of music
from a snare drum. He was with a group of novices in
the middle of the quad. A large square meadow. On
one side was their church, which they called the sanctum. There was the schoolhouse on another. Adjacent
to that was a playground. The fourth side was the wellness building. A series of trailers where the counselors and Mercy worked. But he hadn't laid eyes on her
since lunch.

These people were experts at stonewalling and de-
flection. He thought his time in basic training in the
army had been hell. Nope. The Shining Light redefined
the meaning of the word.

Up before sunrise for morning meditation. Followed
by prayer. Then yoga. A cleansing with crystals. Ser-
mons or rather homilies from the great Empyrean and
others. Climbing a tree as a metaphor for ascending to

higher plane. But really, it was just climbing trees for over an hour. Then someone needed an extra hand in the barn, where he had cleaned out stalls and shoveled hay. Of course, there was learning to connect with his soul through singing and movement, better known as dance. Next was balancing and unblocking his chakras through Reiki—an energy healing technique where Harvey, one of the elders, had to lay hands on him. A creepy, older dude with sagging skin who seemed to be touching him for all the wrong reasons.

And that was the word that kept springing to the forefront of his mind about this place.

Wrong, wrong, wrong. Down to how every activity had to be done barefoot, even climbing a tree. Like they were worried a novice would make a break for it, but couldn't because they weren't wearing shoes.

The one good thing was that he had avoided unburdening. All he'd had to say was that he wasn't ready to share. They pushed, altering their techniques, and he kept repeating the single phrase until they stopped.

Sneaking out of the bunkhouse to investigate in the middle of the night had been impossible with guards posted at the front and back. A change in protocol that had started with his arrival according to the novices. Then there had been an emergency drill at two in the morning. A wailing siren had sounded. Everyone got up and gathered behind Light House. For a lecture, about safety and how during a real event that was the meeting point.

He had wondered if the drill was a sleep deprivation tactic directed at him.

Even though he learned nothing weighed on him, his

frustration ticked through him like a time bomb counting down to when this mission blew up in his face. The
worst part was seeing Mercy and not being able to talk
to her. To touch her. To engage in any manner other
than a shared glance because of her father's perpetual
interference.

There were eyes and ears everywhere. Guards constantly on patrol.

He looked around for any sign of Alex or Shawn.
One or the other had been consistently keeping close
tabs on him. Shawn was easier to talk to and had let it
slip he thought the compound got their weapons from
the Devil's Warriors, an outlaw motorcycle club. He
didn't come across as an unreliable source, since he
used to be in the MC, but Shawn didn't seem the most
informed either.

As Rocco whirled in the quad, pretending to empty
his mind to the beat of the drum, he looked past the
wellness building, not letting his thoughts divert to
Mercy. Though she was a tempting diversion from this
new kind of hell.

Tamping down his annoyance, he focused past the
quad on the security building.

He'd only been inside once, to meet others on the
team, and for a brief tour that included passing by a restricted area, where Rocco needed to venture. Then he'd
been hurried out and handed over to Harvey.

Speak of the devil. Dressed in yellow, Harvey left his
trailer and set a course straight toward him. For a man
in his senior years, he had quite the spring in his step.

Rocco groaned as Harvey stopped beside the drum-
mer and swayed to the beat with his gaze transfixed on

im, a wide gap-toothed grin melting over his leathry face.

The music finally stopped.

Eden, the counselor who had led the session, raised er palms. "You did a glorious job. I am so privileged o help you on this journey. I hope our time together as not only grounded you, but also freed you. May you eel more connected with your soul and one another. Go and walk with the Light today."

Everyone clapped.

Harvey rushed over to him.

Tipping his head back to hide the roll of his eyes, Rocco raked a hand through his loose hair and sucked n a deep breath.

"You were beautiful in motion," Harvey said.

"Thanks, man." Rocco picked up his Stetson, socks and shoes and started walking to Mr. Touchy-Feely's trailer.

Harvey put a hand on his shoulder and kneaded the muscle. "You're so big and strong. But also, very tight. Your musculature is exquisite. The tension in the fibers, not so much. It's quite disconcerting. I'm getting the sense you must be feeling a great deal of stress, and this is how it's manifesting. As though you were under immense pressure. Your burdens don't have to be carried alone. Our family is here for you, my brother. I was thinking that we could incorporate some massage into our Reiki session today. Help loosen you up."

"Nope." Rocco removed the counselor's hand that was wandering around his trapezius muscle and put on his cowboy hat. "Massage isn't necessary. I just need to go for a run."

"Open yourself to the process. You should try it. Everyone says I have magic hands. The commune rave about my Reiki massage therapy. Five stars." Harvey held up his hand, fingers spread wide. "I kid you not." He pressed his palm to Rocco's back and rubbed.

"I'm not ready for all the touching. It makes me fee too…" He searched for the right word. "Vulnerable."

Harvey's eyes brightened and he pushed his glasses up his nose. "But it is through sharing our vulnerability that we grow."

"Yeah, man, I'm not ready."

Mercy's trailer door swung open, and she stepped out Lovely as ever in a white sundress and her hair pinned up in a loose bun.

Please, save me. But he had no idea how that could happen.

Smiling, she waved as she approached them. "Harvey, there's a change in the schedule for today. You're going to do a Reiki session with Louisa." She made eye contact with one of the novices on the quad and beckoned to her. "And I'm going to work with Rocco," she said. Harvey's mouth opened, the protest clear in his eyes. "This is the only break in my schedule where I can fit in a training session. You're such a generous soul, I know you understand."

Rocco put on his socks and shoes.

"Um, yeah, I guess so." Harvey gave an uncertain nod.

"I appreciate your cooperation," she said, patting his arm.

This was a side of her he rarely saw. Soft but firm, unapologetic and direct, confident yet kind. Everything a leader should be. No wonder he was enamored with her.

"Please tell our guest here," Harvey said, gesturing to Rocco, "how healing my Reiki massages can be."

"On a scale of one to five?" Mercy lifted her hand. "Five stars. He can correct any energy blockages in our life force if you give him a chance. The tension will melt from your body."

Harvey beamed. "See. I told you. Tomorrow, we'll try it." He put an arm around Louisa and guided her to his trailer.

Mercy started walking and he followed.

"Thank you," Rocco said, his voice low. "He makes me uncomfortable."

"Reiki isn't for everyone." She quickened her step. "Harvey can be effusive and affectionate. Expresses himself through touch. I think my father assigned him to you to get under your skin."

Mission accomplished. "Where are we going?"

"To my second favorite spot on the compound."

He was about to ask what was her first when she grabbed his hand, and they took off running. The moment was light and carefree, and he just wanted to go with it.

They ran past huts and tiny houses where couples and families lived, passing the infirmary, and darted into a grove. The trees were fifty feet tall and had clusters of green fruit. The air was spicy and fragrant.

"What grows here?"

"Black walnuts. My father had this grove planted when I was a child because I'm deathly allergic to peanuts, which he banned from the compound." She stared up at the nuts in the trees. "They'll be ready to harvest in a couple of weeks. We'll do it during the waxing moon, then we'll make black walnut butter for the year, which is delicious, especially with a little lavender honey."

"I thought if you were allergic to one nut you were allergic to all."

"That is a common fallacy. I was tested for allergies." She took his hands, interlacing their fingers. "Did you know peanuts aren't actually a tree nut? Their legumes."

Learn something new every day. "Had no idea."

She stared at him with patient, tender gravity that had devastated him from the first. He couldn't bear the thought of anything ever hurting her, much less killing her. The world was a better place because she was in it.

A breeze blew wisps of hair that had fallen loose from her bun. The golden strands brushed her face and he ached to touch her cheek and tuck them behind her ear. Why did she have to be so beautiful? There was something ethereal about the delicacy of her porcelain skin, and the arresting mix of her electric blue eyes and sunny blond hair. And her heart was so open, so strong and full of light. Why did she have to be everything he never knew he wanted and couldn't have?

Focus. You've got a job to do.

Rocco tore his gaze from hers and glanced up at the sky. "I've heard people talking about the upcoming full moon. But I don't get what the lunar cycle signifies to you all," he said, looking back at her.

"Well, new moons are a time to initiate beginnings. That's when we accept novices. We plant seeds for the future and set clear intentions for the month ahead. Full moons are about transformation when the seeds of the new moon come into bloom. We hold shedding ceremoies and people are reborn as Starlights. But this one, on Tuesday, is different."

Rocco drew her closer, bringing her flush to his body, and he heard her breath catch. The sexy sound quickened his blood, awakening every cell in his body "Different how?"

"Because of the eclipse."

He'd spent so much time during their training sessions learning about her, what made her tick, what made her smile and laugh, made her uneasy or blush, for the sake of digging deeper into her cult that he was at a disadvantage.

"How does a lunar eclipse change things?" he asked.

"It'll be a full eclipse. A supercharged version. Like a wild card, bringing volatility and exposing secrets. A time for one thing to end and something else to begin. The moon will be directly opposite the sun. There could be friction, intensified emotion, polarity. My father wants us to be cautious."

"Are you worried about something bad happening?"

"No." She shook her head. "We'll do a cleansing ritual that night and have a shedding ceremony. Things will be revealed, but whatever happens is meant to."

She amazed him. She had so much faith in how things would work out. "Don't you ever worry?" Unable to stop himself, he brushed her hair back behind her ear, caressing her skin. Keeping her close, he watched the flush creep up on her cheeks.

Mercy pressed closer. One small hand curled over his shoulder, up his neck, her fingers diving into his hair. Her other hand moved up his back, her fingers dancing over each vertebra, leaving a trail of sensation in their wake.

He could lose himself in her. Even scarier, he wanted to.

"You saw me have a panic attack," she said. "That's proof I worry."

She stared up at him, and he was aware of every inch of her that made contact with his body. The roundness of her hips. The softness of her curves. Her smile. Her smell—she smelled so good, vanilla and sunshine. Everything about her triggered a visceral response.

There was something here, between them, electric and charged, that neither of them could probably afford to explore. But that didn't curb his desire, no, his need to hold her. To kiss her.

A low, husky hum came from her, as though she were giving consent, the sound shooting down low in his belly. She rose on her toes, angling her mouth toward his, giving him a clear green light.

He lowered his head to hers, aching to taste her.

A horse whinnied, a rider approaching, and they jumped apart, separating like teenagers.

Chapter Six

Mercy's heart hammered in her chest as Shawn rode up on horseback.

What had she been thinking to get so close to Rocco? What if her father had seen them together, her body pressed up against his, lost in the feel of him, that manly musky scent of his curled around her right along with his arms?

She hadn't been thinking at all. Just feeling.

Feeling reckless and sensual. Hungry for his touch.

Well, she had been thinking a little, enough to assume this was a good spot where they wouldn't be seen. Someone must have watched them come here after they left the quad. She couldn't even get ten minutes alone with him in a black walnut grove when she wanted a solid hour behind a locked door in a bedroom. Which would never happen here on the compound.

But this was more than lust or hormones or chemistry, whatever she called it. He was able to soothe her. She could take care of herself, so used to hiding her unhappiness and unease. It was nice not to have to with him. Nice to have strong arms around her when she was shaken. To have someone to really talk to. They'd

shared so much. Talked about their childhoods, thei
disappointments, their dreams. She wanted the Shir
ing Light to branch out. To open a store in town tha
she'd manage, selling their honey, soaps, artwork. Sh
wanted to make candles, too.

That was what was so powerful about what she ha
with Rocco. She trusted him with her story, with her pair
with her hopes, and he trusted her enough to do the same

She'd thought being on the compound with him woul
bring them closer together, but everyone was conspirin
to keep them apart.

Shawn was almost within earshot.

"I haven't had a minute to myself," Rocco whispered
with his back to the inbound rider. "I could really us
some time to process all the lessons, try to open my
chakras."

She wanted to respond, but Shawn was already o
top of them.

He reined in his horse and slid off his mount. "The
need some help at the barn, Rocco, cleaning out stalls.

"I can go to the barn," Mercy said. "I've already aske
him to take care of something else."

"No," Shawn said, shaking his head. "That won'
be necessary. I don't think Empyrean would want yo
to do that."

"Could you go handle that issue for me?" Mercy
tipped her head to the side, giving Rocco the go-ahea
to get out of there, and he didn't hesitate to leave. "Since
I have you here, Shawn, I'd like to go over some security concerns that I have."

"With me?" His horse neighed. "Shouldn't you talk
to Alex or your father?"

"I see such promise in you." Mercy smiled. "I'd rather lk to you." She shifted her gaze, watching Rocco hur- ing away. She loved the way he moved—the long, im- tient strides tempered by a sort of sauntering grace. ie appreciated everything about him, down to the way : wore his jeans, low on his hips, the faded fabric ashed to a softness that outlined the sinewy muscles of s legs. "Unless you don't think you're up for the task," ie said to Shawn, unable to take her eyes off Rocco, :citement still rippling over her skin from touching m and being touched by him.

"Of course I am. Whatever I can do to be of service," iawn said.

Smiling, Mercy refocused on the man in front of her give the man she was completely falling for a chance catch his breath alone.

OCCO SLIPPED INSIDE the security building.

His timing was perfect. The others were patrolling ie grounds and practicing at the firing range on the ir end of the compound. That was probably why they ther had him on lockdown with Harvey or out at the irn shoveling manure around now.

He darted through the building, passing the offices, iunge and bay of computers, heading straight for the estricted area. Reaching the locked door, he pulled out is kit that was strapped to his ankle.

Rocco opened the set of lock-picking tools and at- icked the pin tumbler. He slipped the L-shaped part ito the cylinder to keep pressure on the pins. Next, he id the straight piece into place and searched for the ght angle to access the locking mechanism. He had tackled this kind of lock before and estimated it wou[ld] take him thirty seconds tops.

One tumbler clicked into place, then a second an[d] third. He worked on the next two. Finally, the last pi[n] gave way and the tumbler fell into place.

He opened the door and ducked inside, closing [it] behind him.

The breath whooshed out of him at what he saw[.] Racks of assault rifles—M16s, HK416s, SIG 550s[,] semiautomatic sniper rifles with scopes, a variety o[f] pistols, cases of ammo, bulletproof vests. Hundred[s] upon hundreds of weapons.

He hurried through the space, mentally cataloging[] what he could. His primary focus was on the type o[f] ammo they had beyond caliber: full metal jacket, hollow point, soft point.

No armor-piercing. At least not here.

No sign of any destructive devices. No grenades, n[o] RPGs, no explosives.

There was one unopened wooden case in the back with a lightning bolt burned into the wood. He thought of the stickers on the bumper of the truck that had run Dr. Tiggs off the road. A white lightning bolt on a red background. This mark was black.

He'd seen the white bolt while thumbing through their books in the sanctum as he listened to Empyrean's homily.

Was this yet another case of weapons for them when they already had enough to arm every man, woman and child here twice over? Or was this case meant to be shipped?

Percy had told him that they'd gotten it wrong.

aybe the Shining Light didn't have a weapons sup-
ier. Maybe they were the arms dealers.

He got up and hurried through the rows of weapons
the door. But when he opened it, Alex was standing
the other side, grinning, with three more guards for
ckup.

MARSHALL LAY IN BED, his need thoroughly sated, his
ody agreeably tumbled and lazy from his afternoon
elight with Sophia.

The shower stopped in the en suite. Once she dressed
nd he sent Sophia on her way, he'd clean up. Go for a
ong ride on his stallion, Zeppelin.

There was a light rap on the door.

He groaned, hating to be disturbed when he was in
is private quarters. "One minute."

Rolling out of bed, he grabbed his white silk robe
nd slipped it on, tying it closed. He checked his face
n the mirror, brushed his hair in place. His gaze fell to
is tattoo of the Shining Light on his chest.

All he had to do was stay the course and his empire
vould keep growing, expanding. Twenty novices would
)e reborn during the next ceremony. The most they've
ever had at one time.

Nothing—and no one—was going to get in his way.

He went to the door and opened it.

"Empyrean." Alex bowed his head. "I'm sorry to
disturb you."

Better now than twenty minutes ago. "What is it?"

His gaze lifted and a smile spread across his face.
"You were right. Rocco broke into the restricted area

in the security building. I found this on him." Alex hel
up a lock-picking kit.

The cowboy came prepared. "That didn't take long
I would've given him a week. Did anything turn up o
him under the name Kekoa?"

"Nothing."

"No matter. This transgression will be enough
Where is he now?"

"Handcuffed in one of the unburdening rooms."

"Perfect. Dose his dinner with ayahuasca. Once i
kicks in, we'll get to the bottom of whatever he's up
to." He wouldn't be able to hide anything while he was
drugged.

"Then what?" Alex asked.

Marshall needed to get rid of that agent of chaos.
This was his chance, but it had to be done right. "De-
pends on what he says." His thoughts careened to his
daughter. "Tonight, you and Mercy should try bundling," he said, referring to the practice of sleeping fully
clothed with another person during courtship. The point
was to create a strong, intimate bond before marriage.
"She needs more encouragement to see v̱ŏ." ʰᵉʳ future husband. To take this prᵒᶜ̌closed the door and

"Yes, sir. I lookf̧ᵒʳ the bathroom dressed, and a
"Ofᵤₗisteningᵗᵒ him.
ᵧknowing the answer. He asked, striding toward her,
ₛₕₑ'd lie. He merely wanted to see

She hesitated, debating. "Yes. I didn't mean to. I asn't trying to eavesdrop."

Not this time. He slid a hand around the nape of her eck and tugged her to him. "Do you remember the lesson I taught you about discretion and loyalty?"

Sophia stiffened, her face flushing.

He'd taken a riding crop to her bare bottom. He made ertain all his lessons were unforgettable.

"Yes." She trembled. "I won't say anything."

Oh, but she would. "I need you to be of service. To o what you're so good at."

Confusion swept across her face. She lowered to her knees and reached for his robe.

"No, not that." Sighing, he snatched her up by the arms. "The reason I had to teach you a lesson to begin with."

"I don't understand."

"Sit and I'll explain."

Chapter Seven

Finished with her updates to the lesson plans for th
children who were homeschooled on the compound
Mercy was pleased with all she had accomplished in :
couple of days. She'd integrated weekly art, music and
movement/dance classes after weeks of coordinating
with the creatives, as well as finding someone to star
a soccer program. Her father had opposed organized
sports for years, claiming it led to unhealthy competition and division. She'd been advocating for it to nc
avail until now.

Of course, she couldn't help but wonder if her speech
about focusing on development, working together and
exercise rather than winning, as well as her detailed
plan to ensure the children rotated on teams had finally
persuaded him.

Or if it had been Rocco's presence on the compound
that had pushed him to give her what she wanted. Another tether tying her to the Shining Light.

She closed her eyes and fantasized what it would be
like to be free of her autocratic father and obligations
to her community. To her family.

Guilt seeped to the surface. Then she saw Rocco.

is sexy smile. His kind eyes. And a warmth, a sense serenity, washed away her shame.

Urgent pounding rattled the office door, startling ercy. Before she could get a word out, Sophia burst side the room.

"Thank the Light I found you." Sophia shut the door nd hurried over to the desk.

"What's wrong?" Mercy jumped to her feet. "Is it y father? Is he okay?" Ever since she was a little girl hen someone had taken a shot at him, she'd always orried about his safety and well-being. After that day, ey built a wall around the compound. But it didn't stop er from fretting that a novice would infiltrate under alse pretenses and hurt him. Or as their numbers sky-ocketed that the responsibility of caring for so many vould give him a heart attack.

"No, it's not about your dad," Sophia said, and relief eeped through Mercy. "It's Rocco. He's been locked up in one of the unburdening rooms."

Mercy's thoughts stalled along with her breath for a moment. "Why? What happened?"

Shaking her head, Sophia shrugged. "I don't exactly know. I think Alex caught him nosing around where he didn't belong. But I overheard your father saying that they're going to dose him later, then find out what he's up to."

Dose him?

The movement's use of ayahuasca, a powerful drug, was only for their religious ritual during the rebirth of a novice. The person would willingly consume it be-fore unburdening to Empyrean in private. Then in a ceremony in front of the entire community that per-

son would claim their new first name and becom
Starlight.

Mercy had never been under the influence of
drug, but her father had explained that there was
way for a person to hide anything while on it.

But sacred tonic was never forced on someone. T
violated what they believed in.

"Maybe you misheard my father," Mercy said,
wanting it to be true.

"I'm certain of what I heard. After they force Roc
to unburden, your dad plans to punish him for whatev
he did wrong. Flagellation."

Bile rose in the back of Mercy's throat.

Their practices might seem antiquated, even harsh,
those on the outside, but as a result, they had a peacef
commune. A collective that loved and helped each oth
This was a utopia to so many. No murder. No rape. N
theft. No community beyond their gates could say th
same, and for that reason their numbers grew each yea

But Rocco was a guest. Not a member of their com
munity bound by their rules and subject to their pur
ishments. This was wrong. "I've got to speak with m
father."

"And once you do, what do you think will happen?
Sophia asked.

Her father would patronize and stonewall her. Migh
even lock her inside her room until he was finished wit
Rocco. Which would be too late to help him.

"You need to get him out of there and off the com
pound," Sophia said as though reading her mind. "Righ
now."

Mercy turned to the top drawer of her desk and en-ed her code in the digital lock. The drawer opened.

grabbed her set of keys that gave her access to most

as and doors, except for any that belonged to her fa-

r.

But something terrible occurred to her. She looked

Sophia, who was watching her expectantly. "Why

you come here to tell me all this?"

The notion that this could be a setup, contrived to

Mercy in trouble and drive a wedge between her

d her father, couldn't be dismissed.

"You've never liked me, have you?" Sophia asked.

There was no regard or even shared interests be-

een them. That was a truth Mercy had not bothered to

le. Sophia came to them as Enid Stracke, aka Candy,

unkie and a stripper. Mercy was not one to judge

r previous profession or her addiction, but she hadn't

ken kindly to how the woman, only two years her se-

or, had ingratiated herself with Empyrean. Climbing

to his bed as soon as she had been reborn.

And Mercy hadn't been blind to the fact that her fa-

er had taken advantage of this woman, lost and sus-

ptible, empty and longing for something to fill that

id, replacing what she had left behind in the outside

orld.

The reality of Sophia and her father being together

pulsed her.

"It's not that I don't like you," Mercy said. "It's that

don't trust you. What's your angle? What do you get

ut of helping me?"

Sophia came around the desk and stepped in front of

er. "We're going to be family, and I don't mean in the

sense of the commune family." She took Mercy's ha
and placed it on her stomach. "I'm pregnant."

The words hit Mercy like a physical blow. She ree
back, pulling her hand away.

"I know you'll never look at me as a stepmom, I
maybe we can be sisters." Tears glistened in Sophi
eyes. "Or at least friends. I'm telling you all this to sh
you that you can trust me. I can be Empyrean's w
and be on your side."

Mercy's stomach roiled and it was all she could
not to roll her eyes. She might not remember her de
mother, but she did know that Sophia was no substitu
This was not the time to think about her father man
ing this woman, so she shoved the image aside. "Pro
I can trust you."

The woman's eyes brightened as her tears dried u
"How?"

"Create a distraction for me. Something to draw t
attention of security." If Sophia agreed, then they'd
in this together, both culpable of helping Rocco escaj

"Okay." Sophia took her hand again. "But if I do
promise me that we'll be sisters."

Not all sisters had a harmonious relationship. Fro
the stories the novices had shared with her, some fai
ilies barely tolerated one another. But she understo
what Sophia was asking—to be Empyrean's queen a
have the princess fall into line with the new world ord

Mercy never imagined she'd be the type to sell h
soul for anyone's favor or help, but the one thing sl
wanted even less than playing nice with Sophia was f
her father to hurt Rocco. He'd overstepped and ma
a mistake, perhaps out of curiosity. She knew he w

od man, and she refused to believe he'd done any-
g maliciously wrong. This was probably more about
father wanting to demonstrate to her who was in
rge, teaching her a lesson about standing up to him,
g Rocco as a pawn. No matter what he was guilty
she wouldn't stand by and allow him to be drugged
beaten.

'I can promise to be your friend and a sister to your
y," Mercy said, for Rocco and the sake of the un-
n child. She'd grit her teeth, swallow her displeasure
embrace this. No matter how much it sickened her.

Sophia nodded, a smile tugging at her mouth. "Good
ugh for me. Get ready for my signal. I'll need twenty
utes. But that will still leave the guards at the front
back gates."

"They won't matter."

"Once you get to Rocco, how will you sneak him out
he compound?"

They weren't friends yet, and clearly her father hadn't
rusted Sophia with all their secrets.

"Don't worry about that," Mercy said. "Leave it to me.
st hold up your end of this deal."

"I will." Sophia opened the office door and bolted
m the room.

Mercy hauled in steadying breaths, trying to ground
rself. Regardless of her reservations about going
ainst her father's orders, she had to do the right thing
d put a stop to this.

Not wanting to appear as if she was rushing, she
ok her time locking up the office. Her keys jangled in
r trembling hands. She crossed the quad toward the
nctum where they worshipped. Behind the building

were the unburdening rooms that were little more th
modified shipping containers on cinder blocks with c
mate control, stairs leading up to the door and bars
the windows. Each one had a desk, two chairs, a t
let and bed. Sometimes unburdening took hours, bu
always took a toll on the body, requiring undisturb
rest afterward.

Forcing herself to stroll rather than run, she me
tally kept track of every minute that ticked by. The a
was cool and clammy. There would be rain. On the h
rizon, dark gray clouds rolled through the sky over t
town, moving toward the compound. A bad storm w
brewing.

With each step, her pulse quickened. The chan
she was taking, the risk—reputation, retribution, h
father's wrath—was immense.

Out of the corner of her eye, she spotted Alex. H
was on a trajectory headed straight for her like a mayf
drawn to light. Any second he'd be a nuisance, buz
ing in her ear.

Best just to get it over with. The faster the better.

Slowing her pace, she allowed him to intercept he

"Hey, Mercy," Alex said, catching up. "Hold on a mi
ute."

Sighing, she stopped and faced him. He'd alway
been attractive—in an unmemorable way—overzealou
and not quite right for her.

"What is it?" she asked, wondering if he'd have th
decency to mention the incident with Rocco.

"I'm looking forward to spending time with you lat
tonight," he said, and she gritted her teeth at his abi

to disappoint her. "Especially since you got sick last
ht, and it cut our evening short."

Too bad for him she had planned to get a sudden case
ncontrollable nausea yet again. "Let's play it by ear.
e been queasy off and on throughout the day." See-
him triggered it.

She turned to leave, but he caught her by the arm.

"Empyrean thinks we should try bundling tonight."

Mercy had heard whispers of some who had done
re than talk or cuddle in the night, engaging in non-
etrative sex.

Every couple who had bundled, that she was aware
had been quick to marry.

She flashed a tight-lipped smile around the foul taste
ating her tongue. "I'll consider it."

"Your father wasn't making a suggestion. He doesn't
ieve that you're taking this courtship seriously and I
ree with him. Would you prefer your room or mine?"

The audacity of him.

Seething, she let the fake grin slip from her face
d with her fingertips, grazed his Shining Light tat-
) at the base of his throat. "When I was younger, I
s so scared of you. Remember how you'd sneak into
/ room and crawl into my bed?" His was right down
: hall from hers. Empyrean wanted his daughter by
)od and his son by choice under one roof. Always
gether. "Your hands were like fire as you held mine,
ur fingers clinging so tight to me. Back then I used
think that you could never really love someone. A
lliance, sure. But not for a lifetime. You needed too
uch. Approval. Admiration. Validation." It was al-
ays: *look at me, am I good enough, am I special, am*

I worthy? "Because you're weak. And I was right.'
felt good to speak this truth after being pushed so f
and she considered how she'd share the same though
with her father soon.

He clenched his jaw. "My problem has always be
that I love too much. Too deeply," he said through gritt
teeth. "This is going to happen. You and I were alwa
meant to be. The sooner you realize that, the better."

His self-assuredness knew no bounds.

She glanced down at his hand on her arm. "Let n
go," she said, meaning it in more ways than one.

Something predatory sparked in his eyes like he
picked up on her implication. "And if I don't?"

Then she would make him. A quick punch to th
throat should do the trick.

He squeezed tighter, even more possessive, befor
his hand fell, releasing her. "On the full moon, you
father plans to announce my transformation from gra
to white. He also expects us to seal our union by th
end of the year."

Alex would be her father's successor instead of her
She felt like she'd been the one punched in the throat.

But why him? There were others on the council o
elders who were better qualified.

She should have seen her father's plan all along.
Alex's ascendance from gray to white, elevating his
position. Making him her equal before his inevitable
succession. The desire for them to be married, despite
the fact she considered Alex an overbearing brother.

Not a potential husband.

"I guess I'll cross that borderline incestuous bridge
when I come to it." Or burn it to the ground. Either way,

re wasn't going to be any union between them. "As bundling, we did quite enough of that years ago."

Even though it had been innocent then, she would ver share a bed with him again. In any manner. Under y circumstances.

He narrowed his dark eyes. "We were kids. It was 'ferent—"

Gunshots rang out, making her jump. People screamed, spersing and running for cover.

Her head snapped to the side out in the direction the ports had come from—on the east end of the com- und near the farm.

Sophia. Perfect timing with this distraction.

"We'll finish our discussion later." Alex took off as ree more shots resounded.

Whirling, Mercy bolted for the backside of the sanc- im, passing two more guards who were in a flat-out rint toward the gunfire.

She hustled to the bank of Conex trailers, where hawn stood, posted by room number two.

"You have to hurry!" Mercy raced up to him. "Alex eeds as many guys as he can get to help him."

Shawn glanced back at the door of the unburdening oom, as though questioning the order.

Another gunshot pierced the air.

"You better go!" she said.

Giving a curt nod, Shawn put a hand on the hilt of he gun holstered on his hip and dashed off to assist.

She waited until he was out of sight. Then she fum- led through her keys, found the right one and unlocked he door. Her gaze collided with Rocco's angry stare,

and it was as if he stole the air from her lungs with t
one look.

He never failed to take her breath away.

Seated on the cot, Rocco was shackled to the bol
down frame. She hadn't factored in the possibility t
he might be handcuffed.

"Nice to see you," he said, his brown eyes warmi

She shut the door. "I didn't bring a handcuff key

"Give me one of your hairpins," he said, holdi
out a hand.

She plucked a bobby pin from the messy bun s
wore, dropped it in his palm and he got to work. "C
you really unlock it that easily?"

"Sure can. Just have to get it between the ratch
and the ball, the catch mechanism. Disengage the te
and—" The cuff popped open, releasing him. He he
up his free wrist. "I've had practice." He stood a
clutched her shoulders. "What are you doing in her
It's a risky move on your part. I don't want to get y
into any trouble."

"We don't have much time. I need to get you out
here, off the compound."

"Why?"

"I don't know what you did, but my father plans
dose you tonight with ayahuasca. It's a powerful dr
we use for rituals."

"I know what it is."

"If you've got anything to hide, it will come o
while you're under the influence."

His gaze shifted to the floor. His whole body tense

He *was* hiding something. But what? If only she had

ace to find out, but they didn't have minutes to spare
hat discussion.

Afterward, for your transgression," she said, "you'll
eaten."

He rocked back on his heels. "Like hell I will."

While drugged and weakened, they'd restrain him.
ere won't be anything you could do to stop it." But
could intervene now before it got to that point. "You
n't take any vows, agreeing to follow our ways.
're here to learn and understand. The only way to
vent this from happening is to get you off the com-
nd."

"I can't leave."

"Why not?"

A muscle twitched in his jaw, and he looked away
m her again.

Her heart squeezed. What wasn't he telling her?

"If you stay, whatever secrets you have will come
ight. And you will be beaten," she repeated. She
ssed a palm to his warm cheek, not wanting any-
ng bad to happen to him. "I can't say how severely."
t whatever anger Mercy's father had toward her for
recent acts of rebellion he would take out on Rocco.
that she had no doubt. "We're out of time. Decide.
y or go."

She wanted him to choose to be here. With her. But
ep down, she knew that was no longer a possibility
:ause of whatever secret he was harboring.

He raked his hair back and slipped on his cowboy
. "How can you get me out of here?" he asked, and
nething inside of her deflated. "I won't make it to the
e unseen and earlier your father increased security."

"I have a way. We have a bunker beneath Light Hou
There's a tunnel that leads to the woods. I can get y
out there. But we have to be quick."

IN THE STABLE back from his ride, Marshall put Zep
lin in his stall. Years ago, his daughter had asked h
why he'd chosen such an odd name. He'd told her ab
a type of rigid airship named after the German inve
tor Count Ferdinand von Zeppelin instead of telling
the truth. That he called his horse after his favorite ro
band. Led Zeppelin.

There were other truths he kept from her.

Sometimes he thought about letting Mercy have
year away in *penumbroyage*, to experience things su
as the music he loved, like "Stairway to Heaven," to
whatever she wanted, to explore and make mistak
To feel th pain that would inevitably come from th
wicked world.

But he loved her too much to let her stray, even
a little while, and wanted to spare her that darkness.
only she could see that he was protecting her.

The vast majority of children who had been rais
on the compound, like Alex, never sought to wander
question as adults. In fact, they became his most di
hard disciples.

Why hadn't Mercy followed suit? How had he fail
her?

The handheld radio he carried while riding squawke
"Empyrean, this is Alex. Come in."

He took it from his satchel and pressed the butto
"What is it?"

I have Sophia with me at the farm. I had to restrain
"

Horror streaked through him. "Why on earth would
 do such a thing?"

"She managed to take a gun from one of the guys on
security team and started shooting apples in a tree
 talking nonsense."

That didn't sound like Sophia. "Untie her and put her
the radio."

"But, sir—"

"You have the weapon, don't you?"

"Yes, but—"

"Then put her on."

"As you wish."

Marshall left the stable and headed back toward
 ht House while he waited. The path would take him
 se to the farm.

Gun safety was a top priority on the compound. They
 ined everyone how to properly handle, shoot, clean
 d store a firearm. For the life of him, he couldn't un-
 stand what could've possessed her to do such a thing.

"Empyrean," Sophia said.

"Is what Alex told me true?"

"Yes."

"You could've hurt someone by accident." The act
 s beyond ludicrous, complete madness. And danger-
s. "Why would you take a gun and shoot apples?"

"Because Mercy asked me to create a diversion."

He stilled. "Did you do as I commanded?" Did she
 it Mercy by telling her about Rocco, getting her emo-
nal over the thought of flagellation, setting his plan
 motion?

"Yes, my love. Exactly the way you wanted."

"Good girl." Marshall smiled. When the sun set, [would be] rid of that man once and for all. "Did she te[ll] you how she plans to get him out?" he asked.

"She wouldn't say, but she wasn't concerned abo[ut] the gates."

This was worse than he feared. His daughter wa[s] willing to reveal one of their most precious secrets [to] help a stranger escape. "Put Alex back on."

A moment later, his son said, "Sir, is there somethin[g] going on that I should know about?"

"Mercy is headed for the bunker with Rocco to snea[k] him out through the tunnel. You have my permissio[n] to use lethal force." He wanted Rocco dead. It was th[e] only way to end Mercy's infatuation with him.

"Yes, sir," Alex said, and Marshall could hear th[e] grin in his voice.

Alex had been aching to take a shot at Rocco sinc[e] he'd arrived. Now he'd have his chance. He better no[t] blow it.

"Make sure Mercy doesn't get hurt, and, Alex, don'[t] miss."

"I never do."

Chapter Eight

Lightning lit the sky as they made their way to Light House. The clouds were almost black. Rocco fretted about what would happen to Mercy for breaking the rules by helping him.

He should have been worried about the mission. About failing. Getting caught as he tried to get off the compound.

At that moment, his sole concern was for her.

If he could've stayed, he would have. Not only to meet his objective, but to spare her from suffering any consequences. He'd never once rattled under fire. Whatever the dangers might be, Rocco was ready for them, but being forced to ingest a drug—legal for religious purposes and illegal under all other conditions—spill his guts and take a beating was not a possibility he could entertain.

In the end, he'd break his cover and have nothing to show for it besides bruises.

What her father had planned for him was brutal and inhumane. To think, the entire commune accepted such practices as normal.

This was supposedly the safest place on the planet

for her, but his protective instincts had been in high gear since he drove through the front gate. Her father stunt with that forced courtship only made the knot his gut tighten. Despite her assurances that he need no worry, that was all he did.

Keeping his head lowered, he scanned the area an glanced over his shoulder.

"Stop looking around," she said. "It's suspicious."

"Where are all the security guards?"

Mercy flashed him a smile. "Preoccupied at the farm with a little distraction."

She was full of surprises.

Instead of entering through the back, they went around the main building. At a side door, Mercy stepped inside first, made sure it was clear and waved him in.

"Is your dad here?" Avoiding a run-in with her father would be ideal. Not that he wouldn't like the chance to punch that man in the face.

"He likes to ride his horse before dinner, but since you've been on the compound, he's varied his schedule. There's no telling where he is now."

She closed the door behind them and locked it.

In the hall, she led the way past a mudroom that had racks lined across the walls for people to set their shoes on after they entered. He'd seen an even larger one near the rear entrance.

Up ahead was the staircase to the second story.

She put her hand to his chest, stopping him. "Wait here," she whispered, steering him into a dim alcove beneath the stairs.

"Where are you going?"

"I need to get something from my room." Her blue

es looked more panicked and desperate than he felt. I'll only take me a minute."

No distraction was going to keep the security team eoccupied indefinitely.

Before he could ask her if they had the time to waste, he was gone, disappearing around the corner like a host.

HIS WAS THE first time Mercy had kept her footwear on inside the main building. Rather than it being an act of efiance, it was one of desperation that felt entirely disrespectful. But they had to move quickly and quietly and couldn't spare precious seconds taking off their shoes.

Mercy raced up the steps on the balls on her feet, holding tight to her keys, not making a sound. She raced down the hall to her room. Slipped inside. Grabbed what she needed from the top of her dresser. She spun around and stopped. Her heart flew into her throat as she came face-to-face with Daisy.

The middle-aged woman kept the private living quarters meticulously clean, as well as her father's office.

Daisy smiled. "Hello. I was just finishing up. I got a late start today because…" Her gaze dropped to the shoes Mercy was wearing and her smile fell, too.

Mercy couldn't help looking down at her sneakers— a blatant sign of rudeness. "Oh, I forgot to take them off. How silly of me."

Daisy cocked her head to the side. "You never forget."

That was true. Great care was taken to keep the house clean. It required little effort or thought to remove filthy shoes and avoid tracking in any unnecessary dirt.

"First time for everything. I was rushing." Then s
wondered if that would lead to more questions. F
starters, why was she in such a hurry? "I'm sorry." S
removed the canvas shoes and held them to her che
along with the other item that she hoped wouldn't
needed. "Please don't tell Empyrean."

"Transparency is the way to the Light. Are you as
ing me to obfuscate?"

Yes. Yes, I am. "No. Of course, not. I want to be th
one to tell him about my transgression." Wearing shoe
in the house would be the least of them today.

Daisy nodded. "All right."

"I'll get out of your way." She went to the door an
squeezed by her. "I really am sorry. I know how har
everyone works to keep things clean. I appreciate you
efforts." Mercy hugged her, sincerely grateful for he
diligence and years of service.

Daisy returned the affection. "Thank you. It's so
nice to hear."

"May the Light be with you."

"And also, with you."

Mercy rushed down the steps with her heart pounding a frantic rhythm against her sternum. She hustled
back to the alcove. "Let's go."

Rocco glanced at her bare feet, but thankfully didn't
ask questions.

They crept through the hall, passing the great library,
a vaulted two-story room, where she had spent thou-
sands of hours as a child, reading and playing hide-and-
go-seek. It was her favorite space in the whole house.
One she would never get a chance to share with Rocco,
like so many other things. She had so hoped this would

an opportunity to let someone she had formed a pow-
ful connection with into her life and world. To build
it. Explore where that bond might lead.

As always, her father was two steps ahead of her,
ing what he could to sabotage any of her efforts that
ntradicted his wishes.

Disappointment sliced through her, but dwelling on it
asn't a luxury she could afford. She had to get Rocco
t of there. That was all that mattered.

Voices, the clatter of dishes and aroma of food being
epared came from the kitchen.

Before reaching the dining hall, she whispered,
They'll begin setting up for supper soon. This way."

She cut down a short corridor that led to the base-
ent, where they kept everyday supplies, and opened
e door. After she slipped on her shoes, they hurried
own the stairs. Those who worked in the kitchen reg-
larly came to the basement, which appeared to be no
ore than six hundred square feet, but they didn't know
vhat else was hidden down there.

At the bottom of the steps, she took his hand in the
itch-black darkness. Not only because she longed to
ouch him, but also for a more practical reason. "I'm
ot going to turn on the light. Not until we reach the
ounker. Just in case anyone passes by upstairs, I don't
want them to get suspicious."

He drew closer and the scent of him curled around
her. Sweaty, pine-laden musk.

"I trust you," he said, his warm, strong fingers tightening around the edge of her hand.

She was aware he hadn't missed the sound of her
sharp intake of breath, but hoped he couldn't hear the

way her heart thudded in response to his touch, to h
proximity.

Whenever they got close, he turned her into a mes
bundle of sensual frustration. No one else did that. Eve
Alex had never even come close.

"Lead the way," he said, his voice low and deep.

Mercy guided him through the dark depths of th
basement, with the heat of his body tickling, teasin
almost pressed against her back. Having him so clos
unable to see and only feel, made her dizzy.

She knew every inch of this house and could mak
her way through blindfolded, if necessary, but Rocc
was a distraction.

Forcing herself to focus, she extended her other arn
They'd reach the far wall soon.

Her fingers grazed cool cement. She turned left. "N
much farther."

A few feet ahead and they came to the last shelvin
unit that was always kept empty.

She placed his hand on one of the steel racks. The
she grabbed onto it as well. "Help me pull it."

Together, they gave it a hard tug. There was a fain
click and the fake wall attached to the shelving unit sli
open with barely a whisper.

She felt her way around to the lever. Yanked down o
it and pulled open the door to the bunker. She steppe
inside, ran her palm along the wall, fumbling for th
switch and flipped on the lights. Fluorescent strobe
flickered and buzzed as they came alive. Everythin
inside Light House drew power from the solar panels
Her father believed in being prepared in the event of a
worst-case scenario.

Rocco entered the bunker.

Quickly, she tugged the faux wall back in place, but n't bother closing the heavy steel door to the bunker. fortunately, she couldn't lock it. Her father had never trusted her with a code to do so. It was possible he s indeed a prophet, a spiritual seer who'd foreseen at she'd one day betray him like this.

But Rocco made her feel—impulsive, reckless, fish—in a good way. He brought out the most intense rsion of herself.

Rocco wandered deeper inside and glanced around, ering at the long gun rack filled with rifles and auto- atic weapons. He took a 9 mm from the wall, pulled ck the slide and peeked inside the chamber.

"Empty," he said.

"They're all unloaded. We store the ammo sepa- tely." She went to the cabinet beside the rack of weap- s and used one of her keys to unlock it.

Rocco grabbed a loaded magazine from one of the any stacks. "I can't believe you have a full armory wn here as well as in the security building." He in- rted the loaded clip into the gun, working the slide chamber the first round.

"The tunnel is this way."

They ran by shelves stocked with nonperishable food: ried beans, rice, jars of preserved fruits, vegetables, ackers, jams and black walnut butter. In another part f the bunker, they had cases of Meals, Ready-to-Eat— ot enough to feed five hundred for weeks—a stockpile f toilet paper, and other essentials. They passed the nall kitchen, toilets, shower rooms and an infirmary at was fully supplied with medicine.

"What's with the bunker?" he asked. "Are you preparing for Armageddon?"

No, they were prepared for a siege. Everyone in the commune believed that if they ever faced any danger it would come from the outside.

"Better safe than sorry. At least that's what my father says. He wants to prevent another Waco from happening here in Wyoming." He'd protect his people at all costs. This was only one measure. "Come on."

She led the way through a large open bay of three-tier high bunk beds that they'd made on the compound. It was the same kind they used in the bunkhouses for novices.

Whenever someone asked what they did with the unaccounted-for extras, her father had told the carpenters that they'd sold them, like their other products that brought in a profit. And some had.

After a couple of turns through an area that was designated as restricted for most of the commune, in the event that they had to use the bunker, they entered the private quarters—another open space for Empyrean, her, Alex, the council of elders and their loved ones.

They reached the door that led to the tunnel.

She slid back the heavy barrel bolt. There was no lock or code on this door in case of an emergency and they needed to evacuate. She pushed it out, opening it. The first set of motion-sensor lights flicked on.

"Follow the tunnel. It goes for less than a mile and will let you out in the woods, closer to town. There are three different paths you can take, depending on where you want to go, but I'd recommend staying off them. If you hurry, they won't be able to intercept you once ey realize you're gone." She gave him the wooden edge she'd taken from her dresser. "It's a doorstop."

On her fourteenth birthday, when her father had declared her a *woman* to the community because she had gotten her first menses, she asked the carpenters to make one for her to keep Alex from slipping into her room. There were no locks on the bedroom door handles to stop someone from getting in. But there were padlock hasps fitted to the outside in case her father wanted to lock either of them in. Something she had never questioned. That was simply the way things were done and she'd never known anything different.

"Use it, just in case," she said. That way they wouldn't be able to follow him through the tunnel.

He stared down at her with such intensity, his eyes burning into hers, and moved closer. A little step that didn't feel little at all. She looked at the pulse beating along the line of his throat, at his chest rising and falling with quickened breaths.

"Mercy," he said, her whispered name sounding like a question on his lips, and an echo in her heart.

He caressed her face, his fingertips diving into her hair that was still pinned up, and bent his head, setting his mouth to hers.

She dissolved on the spot as she kissed him back.

Would she end up in the fiery hell her father preached about for this intimacy with a nonbeliever?

All she knew for certain was that it felt like heaven.

So she silenced the conflicted voice in her head and sank into Rocco. When he parted her lips with his own and slid his tongue inside her mouth, she made a quiet noise of pleasure that was just shy of a moan.

He tugged her even closer, putting a hand at the small of her back. No longer waiting for this delicious moment that seemed as though it would never happen, she put her arms around his neck and pressed her whole body against the muscular landscape of his. All at once, hunger and heat rushed through her. She fisted the back of his T-shirt, pushing up onto her toes, welcoming the sweet slide of his tongue, the heady taste of him filling her senses. He tasted like mint and coffee. He tasted like happiness, and she could not get enough of it. Couldn't get over how he kissed her, as if he were consuming her in such desperate, frantic urgency.

Nipping at his lower lip, she rolled her hips against the hardness bulging between his thighs, unable to stop herself. As though she had been untethered and set free. She didn't want to stop there, at a kiss, and if circumstances were different, she'd get her hands and mouth all over him.

On a groan, he clutched the mass of her hair bundled at her nape and tipped her head back, making her gasp.

"God," she muttered, excitement running in wild molten rivulets through her.

His head whipped to the side as if he'd heard something. Then she caught it—the sound of approaching footfalls in the bunker. Dangerously close. Almost on top of them.

"Go." She shoved him toward the tunnel and her heart cracked like glass splintering in her chest.

"Come with me."

Her breath hitched, blood roaring in her ears. Had she misheard him? "What'd you say?"

"Come with me," he repeated, this time taking her and and pulling her close.

The footsteps grew louder. At least three or four men. ny second they'd enter the restricted area and see them.

If she stayed on the compound, there'd be horrendous onsequences. And if she left with Rocco, there would e uncharted terrain and obstacles and cliffs ahead.

She'd never been so conflicted, so torn in her life.

Alex and three others charged into the enclosed oace.

Pop! Pop!

Gunshots boomed, bullets biting into the concrete all near her head. Rocco moved her out of the line f fire.

"Don't shoot!" Alex ordered. "Mercy's not to be hurt."

Time was up. Her gaze flew to Rocco's hard stare, nd she knew that taking this leap of faith would be worth it.

That he was worth it.

All hesitation evaporated, and she gave him her word-ess answer. Mercy shielded Rocco with her body—Alex ould hit a melon the size of a human head with a sin-le shot from fifteen yards day or night—and scurried ackward, getting them both across the threshold into he tunnel.

Alex stopped running and took aim, but Rocco re-urned fire, forcing the men to take cover.

She met Alex's eyes for a split second, saw the hor-or and anger contort across his face right before she lammed the door closed.

Rocco shoved the wooden wedge under the lip of the loor. Using his foot, he rammed it tight.

He grabbed her hand, and they took off down the tunnel. Along the way, he shot out each light that flashed on, shattering the bulb. Once Alex and the others eventually got the door open, they wouldn't be able to open fire into the darkness without risking hitting her.

A loud banging resounded on the door behind them. Clutching Rocco, she ran faster. As fast as possible.

With each panicked step she took, three things filled her ears—the frenzied beat of her heart in time with the pounding of fists on the door, and Alex's screams.

"Mercy!"

Bang. Bang.

"Mercy!"

Chapter Nine

It was nightfall by the time they made it to the outskirts of town. A downpour had started while they were racing through the woods. Rocco had been impressed with Mercy. Not only had she broken him out of the unburdening room, saving him from being drugged and beaten, but in the bunker, she'd stayed calm, even while Alex's men shot at them. In the woods, she had kept up with the grueling pace he'd set over rough terrain. He'd only had to help her once or twice after the ground had turned muddy and slick. Most surprising of all, she had left with him when it would have been so much easier for her to stay.

The wind and rain continued to buffet them, soaking them through when they reached a small service station—the Dogbane Express. Panting, weary and wet, she had to be physically nearing the end of her endurance. Even though he was already blown away by her fortitude, he hoped she could wring a little more out of herself.

He marched up to the door and pulled it open, ushering her inside first.

"Wow, you two are drenched," the attendant said.

She gazed out toward the empty gas pumps. "Were y⟨
out walking in that storm?" The stocky woman can⟨
from behind the register.

"We were already far out and got caught in it." Roc⟨
glanced around and spotted a pay phone. One of the fe⟨
still in the state. "Is that pay phone in service?"

"Yep. Sure is."

He took out his wallet from his back pocket. The on⟨
item that security hadn't confiscated. Cursing the fac⟨
that his vehicle was still on the compound, he whippe⟨
out a dollar bill and slapped it down on the counte⟨
"Can I get change in quarters?"

The attendant hit a button on the register. The cas⟨
drawer opened with a beep. She set four quarters o⟨
the counter. "It's on me." She pushed the dollar bac⟨
toward him.

"Thanks." He slipped the bill in his pocket an⟨
grabbed the quarters. "I'll be right back," he said t⟨
Mercy.

Keeping an eye on her, he went to the pay phone an⟨
picked up the receiver. There was a dial tone, like the
attendant had said, but he exhaled in relief, nonetheless.

The older woman looked over Mercy from head to
toe. "Are you one of those Starlights from that compound?"

Rocco suspected it was her necklace that gave her
away. He'd never seen her without it.

Shivering, Mercy nodded. "Yes, ma'am."

He put fifty cents in the slot and dialed a taxi company.

"Make a break for it, did you?" the attendant asked
with a curious smile.

"Sort of."

"I'll get you a towel. Feel free to help yourself to some ffee. That's on me, too. It's fresh and it'll warm you
"

"Thank you," Mercy said. She grabbed two cups and led them with piping hot coffee. "That's very kind you."

"I'll go get a couple of towels from the back."

He ordered a cab and then called Charlie. "Hey, it's occo."

"I haven't heard from you since you took off with lercy McCoy. It's been days. Are you all right?"

"Yeah. I'm working."

"With Mercy?" Shock rang in Charlie's voice. "Is she n asset?"

Rocco never discussed work with his cousin. All nis time, she had no idea that he had been cultivating Mercy McCoy as a potential asset. Only that she was he sole client he was willing to work with one-on-one.

Mercy headed toward him, trembling like a leaf, and nanded him a cup of coffee.

He mouthed, *thank you.* "I can't get into specifics ight now. Listen, we're about to take a taxi to a motel." He rattled off the name and vicinity in which it was located. From what he could tell from the outside, the place wasn't a fleabag dump, but it wasn't the Ritz either.

"Why are you going to a hotel? And why are you taking a taxi instead of driving your car?"

"It's a long story. Short version is that folks from the compound might come looking for her at my place. Maybe even at yours, too. You should stay with Brian

for the next few days." He took a long sip of coffe
grateful for the warm liquid sliding down his throat.

"I'm at his house almost every night as it is anyway
won't say we're living together because I've still got n
house, but he's given me two drawers and closet space

Not only had Charlie's relationship with Brian caug
him completely off guard, but the two had gone fro
zero to serious at lightning speed. He wasn't complain
ing. In fact, he was thrilled that his cousin had finally l
someone in behind that steel wall she'd put up aroun
her heart, and for it to be a great, solid guy like Bria
made it even better.

"It might be a good idea to have Brian hang out
USD as well. Some Starlights might try to harass yo
there to find out where Mercy is." Nash should approv
it. They didn't hem and haw when it came to the safet
of their loved ones.

The service station attendant came out from the bac
and handed them both towels.

"Can you bring me some things from my place an
pick up stuff for Mercy?" he asked his cousin. "W
both look like a couple of drowned cats. I could als
use a car."

Charlie sighed. "We've got you covered. I'll let you
use my Hellcat and ride with Brian. See you in a few."
She disconnected.

Rocco went to the ATM and withdrew his daily limi
so he could pay for a room in cash. To be sure they
couldn't be tracked down, he'd get the room under an
alias. Beside the ATM was a rack of prepaid cell phones.
Grabbing one, he wished the attendant had mentioned
that the store carried them earlier.

He went to the register, paid for it and used the ac-
ation card as the taxi pulled up.

T THE MOTEL, Rocco unlocked the door to the room
d let Mercy in. There were two double beds, a mi-
owave, mini fridge and a dank, musty smell. "Sorry
isn't nicer."

He took off his sopping wet Stetson and fired off a
ick text to Charlie.

s Rocco. This is a temp number. We'll be in room 12.

HE ROOM WAS FREEZING. He turned down the air-
onditioning. In the closet, he found an extra blanket
d put it around Mercy's shoulders.

She edged deeper inside with her arms wrapped
ound herself. "I thought I'd get a chance to see where
ou lived."

He would've liked nothing more than to welcome
er into his home. Show her how he lived and all the
ings about himself that he'd hidden. "I'm sure your
ather knows where my house is. He'd only send Alex
nd others to come get you."

"I don't think so. You didn't kidnap me. It was my
hoice to leave the compound."

Things happened quickly with bullets flying. No tell-
ng what version of the story her father had been told.
Regardless, Alex was the type to retaliate. If he thought
e knew where to find Mercy, nothing was going to stop
im from going after her.

The man was either obsessed or in love with her. Ei-
her way, Alex wasn't going to simply let her go.

"You left without permission or claiming *penur* *broyage*. Which means there'll be consequences f you, right?"

Looking lost, she pressed a palm to her forehea "I didn't really think about that when I decided to g with you."

"Regrets?" he asked.

If she had any, rather than letting her have a goo night's sleep, he'd have to get straight to questionin her about what she might know. Any innocent detai could lead to something fruitful. Then he'd drop her a the gates to the compound. Reluctantly say goodbye.

But he hoped she didn't have any remorse about tak ing his hand and getting away from the commune. Eve if it was only for a few days.

She turned to him, her mouth opening to answe when headlights shone in front of the window, draw ing their attention. Car doors slammed and there wa a knock on the door.

Rocco peeled back the curtain and peeked out to be sure.

Charlie and Brian were kissing. She was wearing his black cowboy hat and his hand was pressed to the small of her back. Every time he saw their public dis plays of affection he was surprised all over again as if witnessing it for the first time. Brian was the only man to ever soften his cousin. It was nice seeing them both happy and in love.

He opened the door. "Hey."

Charlie held up two small duffel bags. "Reinforce ments are here." Stepping inside, she shoved one bag into his arms. "Grabbed the essentials for you."

Brian crossed the threshold, bringing in the smell of food with him. He set a white food sack beside the microwave. "Double cheeseburger, fries, hummus sandwich, tomato soup and two salads."

Perfect. "Thanks." Rocco turned to Mercy. "This is Brian, Charlie's significant other."

Mercy held up a shaky hand *hello*.

"You need to take a warm shower and change," Charlie said, handing Mercy the other duffel. "All the toiletries you should need. Also, there are some T-shirts, a sweater, leggings and an old pair of jeans I can't squeeze into anymore and a nightgown. You might have to roll the pants up. The only thing white in there are the T-shirts. Sorry."

"That's okay." Mercy still had that deer in the headlights look. "Thank you."

"What's the situation here?" Charlie asked. "Are you two sharing a room?"

His cousin was brusque, opinionated and ruthless when it came to protecting the vulnerable. She was particularly sensitive to battered women. It turned out that she had made it her mission to help victims of domestic violence get away from their abusers and disappear. With Mercy being embroiled in a cult, it only made sense that Charlie would seek to protect her.

"I'm not letting her out of my sight," Rocco said. Mercy might change her mind in the middle of the night, call the compound, sneak out before he had a chance to find out what she might know. As it stood, she was his best lead. He wasn't going to let her slip away or allow anything to happen to her.

"Mercy, are you comfortable with this arrangement?"

Charlie asked. "Because if you're not, I can stay w
you in here and Rocco can sleep in a different roon

"If you stay, I'm staying," Brian said. "Not with y
ladies, of course."

Mercy clutched the duffel to her stomach. "I'll
fine with Rocco. Really. There's no need for you
stay." Her bright blue eyes found his, and relief seep
through him that she was comfortable being alone w
him.

"I don't fully understand what's going on with y
two," Charlie said, glancing between them. "I though
was one thing and then I found out it's something else
She turned to Mercy. "If you ever decide that you wa
to leave the Shining Light, I don't want you to feel lil
you have to rely on a man to help you. Even if that ma
is my cousin. Who happens to be a good guy. Whateve
you need, a place to stay, a job, anything at all, just as
and it's yours."

Charlie was a formidable person to have on one'
side. Mercy would be able to count on her, no matte
what. He wanted her to have as much support as pos
sible with whatever decision she made, but he intende
to make it clear that he wanted to be there for her, too
as much as she'd allow.

"That's incredibly generous of you," Mercy said
"I'm not sure what I'm going to do yet, long-term, bu
thank you."

Charlie gave her a warm smile and then she turned
an icy stare on him. "I need to speak with you privately."
She marched outside, leaving the door open.

Rocco stepped out onto the walkway and shut it.
"Don't come in hot with me. I'm not in the mood."

Rocking back on her heels and putting her hands on hips, she swallowed the words that seemed to be ning on her tongue. She took a deep breath. "Mercy y not have been physically abused, but she's been iso- ed from the outside world, under the strict rule of her ner, where every facet of her life has been controlled. e's in a vulnerable position right now."

"I'm aware."

"Don't take advantage of it."

"Who do you think I am?" She was treating him e he was a stranger and not the blood relative she'd own up with.

"I think you're one of the good ones, but you're still guy. Open your bag."

He unzipped the duffel he was holding. On top of s clothes were condoms. What in the hell? "I'm not a date. I'm working on a mission."

"Call it whatever you want. I've seen how she looks you. It isn't one-sided. Tell me I'm wrong and I have othing else to say."

Irritation sliced through him. Partly because she was ight. Partly because he was wet, cold and starving. "I an be a professional regardless of my personal feel- ngs." And if for some reason he slipped, he always kept n emergency condom in his wallet. He didn't need her o meddle. "This discussion is done. Are we clear?"

"Crystal." She reached into her pocket, pulled out her keys and tossed them to him.

"Thank you for coming so quickly." He marched back inside and found Brian standing alone.

"She's in the bathroom," Brian said, keeping his voice low, and it was then that Rocco caught the sound of the shower running. "Did you learn anything c crete?"

Rocco shook his head. "But I think she might kn more than she realizes. I'll talk to her in the morni after she's gotten some rest. If I come up with nothi I'll pursue a tip that the Devil's Warriors might have in with the weapons supplier." He couldn't count or going anywhere. The lead was threadbare.

Brian unhooked his holstered weapon from his h and handed it to Rocco. "I'll leave you to it. If you do make headway, Becca will want to give it a go."

"Yeah, I figured."

"I understand that it might be difficult, especial after whatever you two just went through," Brian sai gesturing to the bathroom, "but you can't go easy c her. You've got to push hard for answers. *Tonight*. W only have two days left."

No one needed to remind him what he was alread painfully aware of—that they were almost out of time "I got it covered."

"Nash wants to see you first thing in the morning And so that you know, I'll be at USD all day tomor row with Charlie. I won't let anything happen to her."

That went without saying. Rocco not only trusted Brian with his life, but Charlie's as well.

Brian clasped a hand on his shoulder and gave him a sympathetic look before leaving.

The water stopped running in the bathroom. A minute later, Mercy opened the door and steam wafted around her. She stepped out, wearing a tee and black leggings. He couldn't help but notice that she didn't have a bra on.

*Get a grip. You're more than a man. You're an ATF
agent.*

"You should eat," he said, diverting his gaze. "I'm
going to clean up." He hurried past her into the bathroom and closed the door.

Hanging from the shower rod were her bra and panties. The sight of them was a jarring reminder that she
wore nothing under her clothes.

With a firm shake of his head, he snapped himself
out of it and started the water.

If he could've eaten while he showered, he would
have. He zipped through cleaning up, soaking up the
warmth from the hot water, and threw on a T-shirt,
boxer briefs and sweatpants.

In the bedroom, Mercy had placed a spare blanket
on the floor and set out the food like a picnic. She sat
cross-legged, waiting for him.

"I told you to eat. I know you're hungry."

"I've always eaten with my family."

She looked so fragile, fresh-faced with pink cheeks
and a gentle smile.

To call her vulnerable was an understatement. All
of this was new to her, from wearing anything besides
white to eating outside her commune. He would have
given anything to wait until the morning to tell her the
truth, but Brian was right.

He sat beside her. "Do you want half of my burger?"
He wasn't sure offering it was being nice or offensive.

Frowning, she shook her head. "Just because I'm
not on the compound doesn't mean I want to eat meat."

What did it mean, then? She wasn't ready to give up
the ways of her commune, but she was out beyond the

compound with him for a reason. "Do you want to s.
your blessing?"

"Yes." She took his hand. "Thank you for the gift
this meal to sustain us. May it nourish our bodies a
fuel our ability to make this a better world. And than
you for keeping Rocco safe."

Not only had she included him, but she'd cut th
blessing short, leaving out the bits that had secretl
made him uncomfortable.

He stared down at her small hand resting on hi
Soaked in how good it felt. Too good. He looked u
and met her blue eyes. Neither of them said a word
The moment stretched out, thinning until it snapped
Then it was over.

She tried the soup first and next tasted the sandwich
while he dug into his burger and fries. He had to force
himself not to inhale the food and slow down. Even
taking his time, he finished before she'd gotten to the
second half of her sandwich.

"Why did you leave with me?" he asked, needing
to know what this was about for her. Whatever she
needed—time, freedom, space, a new life—he wanted
to make sure she got it.

Putting her sandwich down, she shrugged. "I wanted
to make sure you got away safely and…" Her voice
trailed off as she shifted, facing him. She cupped his
cheeks in both hands, brushing his goatee with her
thumbs. "I wasn't ready to say goodbye."

The scent of her—clean and sweet—tempted him
to draw closer.

But she was the one to move in. She swallowed hard,
then slid her hands into his damp hair. Pulled his head

ward hers, taking his mouth in a tentative kiss—a osting of lips that sent his heart instantly throbbing.

He longed to curl his arms around her, sinking into e feel of her. To drag her against him, lie her down on e bed and plunder. He longed to touch her soft skin d find out if she smelled so good all over. Longed see her eyes grow dark with desire and heavy with tisfaction.

He wanted her to be his.

But he held very still, absorbing her nearness, even ough his body vibrated from the effort of holding ack. This was more than an itch to be scratched. He'd cratched itches in the past and had been fulfilled.

This was different.

She was different.

Finally, his better sense took over. Rocco broke the iss and lowered her hands away from him. "I'm sorry. can't."

She closed her eyes. "Why not?" Her voice was barely a whisper. She looked confused, ashamed and it made his heart hurt.

That moment of physical connection, as slight and tender as it had been, was more than enough spark to jump-start his engines. Swearing silently, he cursed that Charlie was right.

He'd thought about being with Mercy, like this, alone and away from the USD or the compound, but in his wildest dreams he never imagined he'd be the one saying *no*.

"Mercy, look at me." He waited until she'd opened her eyes, and he saw desperation tangled with raw yearning. "There are things I need to tell you."

Soberly, she nodded. "Just tell me."

He dreaded saying the words, knowing that she w
going to hate him for it. "I'm an agent with the Bure.
of Alcohol, Tobacco, Firearms and Explosives. I us
you to get onto the compound to investigate your fath
and the Shining Light."

Chapter Ten

...nable to breathe, Mercy listened to the jarring words ...mbling out of Rocco's mouth. The more he said, re-...rring to her as an *asset*—talking about ghost arms, ...plosives, something horrible happening on the full ...oon—the stronger the brutal sensation inside her, like ...e had walked unsuspecting into the street and a truck ...ad slammed into her, shattering every bone and break-...g her heart into a million pieces.

He stopped talking. Or had finished.

It was quiet in the room for a long time. But ev-...rything hadn't quite penetrated. She couldn't move. ...ouldn't speak.

He stepped forward into her space, the delicious ...smell of him strengthening, and her body tightened to ...guard against it. "Mercy, are you all right?"

She blinked once. Hot tears streaked down her face.

He reached for her. She scurried back and to her feet. Moving away from him, she kept shuffling in retreat until her spine was pressed into a corner. "None of it was real. Everything you told me was a lie."

Rocco got up. "What I feel for you is real. It has been since I first laid eyes on you." Blowing out a heavy

breath, he raked a hand through his hair and pac
around the room.

She cataloged the breadth of his shoulders, the da
strands at the nape of his neck, the way the tendons
his forearms shifted. She felt so much for him that she
endangered herself to spare him any pain.

While she meant nothing to him. He'd only be
using her. To betray her family.

"I omitted more than I lied, but so much of what I'
told you is the truth," he said. "You have to understar
why I couldn't be transparent."

"Because you think we're domestic terrorists."

She'd let him into the compound, shared their secret
showed him they were peaceful and only interested i
making the world a better place and the entire time he
father had been justified in not trusting him.

"I don't think that you or most of the people in you
commune are."

Horror filled her at the implication. "But my father?"

"What does he need with all those weapons?"

"To protect us. From people like you. In the even
one day you decide to attack us."

"Don't lump me in with every other agent." His voice
turned gentle and his eyes pleading. "There are laws
preventing such a thing. The task force would never lay
siege to the compound without just cause."

Oh, no. There was a whole task force? "Tell that to
all the people who didn't make it out of the Waco mas-
sacre." The siege left seventy-five people dead, including women and children.

Rocco shook his head. His frustration was stamped
on his face. "Agents had a legitimate search and arrest

rant that they attempted to serve," he said, and she
ed her eyes. "Mistakes were made in Waco. Agen-
s have studied it, learned from it. No one wants a re-
t of that tragedy." He eased closer. "I would never
something like that happen on my watch. I swear it."

"What do you want from me?"

"We need to know who the Shining Light's weap-
s supplier is and what your father has planned in two
ys when there's a full moon."

All his questions about the moon and what it meant
me rushing back to her. "There's nothing planned be-
les the shedding ceremony." When Alex would shed
ay and don white. When any grievances, ill feelings
hidden transgressions would be released in exchange
r the Light's favor. "I've already told you that."

"You're Empyrean's daughter. You must know some-
ing," he said so harshly that she jumped. A look
ossed his face as if he regretted it. "Please, tell me
hat you know."

This was like a bad dream. She couldn't believe this
vas happening. "My father would never hurt people."

"An informant of mine died in my arms. The last
hing he told me was that your father is behind whatever
s about to happen. Please try and think. You must know
omething that can help stop it and save innocent lives."

A sickening feeling welled inside her. "Don't you
hink that if I knew about an attack my father was planning that I would do everything in my power to prevent it?"

His features softened. "Of course I do. But there is
a plan for something big, something awful to happen
that day."

She shook her head. "I don't know anything about that."

"What about the weapons?"

"My father and Alex handle all the purchases." She was kept in the dark about so much, too much, for so long. "I don't know who the supplier is."

"Where does the money come from? To pay for all?"

Mercy wrapped her arms around her stomach. "My father started the Shining Light with his own money. From a trust fund. It's how he bought the land and had the facilities built. When people choose to become Starlights, they sign over their worldly possessions to the commune. Most of the time, people come to us with nothing."

"But there are some who come to you with quite a lot."

Lowering her head, she said, "Yes." She had questioned her father about how some novices had been recruited. Almost as though their wealthy families had been targeted for showing a weakness that the great Empyrean could exploit. Promises of saving a wayward teen, cleaning up an addict, taking someone drowning in darkness and turning them to the light was powerful. But combined with her father's charismatic personality, it was priceless.

She'd seen him at work firsthand.

The answers he'd given her had been lies. She wasn't blind or silent to the imperfections of their commune, or her father, but that didn't make them terrorists.

"There must be a money trail," Rocco said.

"I was never given access to any accounts or docu-

ntation showing how much there is or where it all
s." God, she didn't even have her own bank account.
e'd had to beg her father to pay for training sessions
the USD. "What are you going to do now? Issue a
rrant to go through my father's computer? Seize his
nk accounts?"

"No. It doesn't work like that." He scrubbed a hand
er his face. "There's no legal basis for one, and even
there was, it would take time that we don't have.
aybe if I can track down the supplier, whoever it is
ight know what's in the works. If they sold your fa-
er explosives, he might have mentioned what it was
oing to be used for."

May the Light help me...and guide Rocco.

After everything she'd told him, he still believed
hat her father was capable of masterminding a deadly
ct of terrorism.

"How are you going to find the supplier?" That might
e the only way to vindicate her father and protect the
ompound.

"The Devil's Warriors."

The outlaw motorcycle club?

All her emotions seesawed from anger to concern.
For Rocco. "They're dangerous. Violent." The commune had a former gang member, Shawn. He had been
looking to escape the never-ending cycle of brutality.
To this day, the horrific things he'd shared sickened and
terrified her. "You can't go to them," she said, stepping
out of the corner toward him.

He plunked down on one of the beds. Resting his elbows on his thighs, he dropped his head in his hands.
"It's my last option."

Her heart squeezed tight in her chest. "You were a most dosed and beaten on the compound because yo got caught snooping around." She sat on the other be opposite him. "If you go to those vicious monsters ask ing about their supplier, they'll kill you."

"I'm not used to assimilating in places like the com pound. But a deadly biker gang?" He shrugged. "I'm used to dangerous territory. That's different."

Was it?

Getting a person to lower their guard took patience and time. Months in her case for her to feel at ease shar ing with him, confiding in him, trusting him. Falling for him.

He must have pushed too hard and too fast on the compound for her father to react the way he had. With time running out, only two days left, why wouldn't he take the same approach with the Devil's Warriors?

He was going to get himself hurt. Or killed. Despite her anger and disappointment with him, something in side her broke, thinking of that possibility.

"I bet you're kicking yourself for wasting too much time on me," she said, "since I turned out to be useless." *Empyrean's daughter.* Rocco had probably thought he'd struck gold.

What a sad joke.

He raised his head, his serious eyes meeting hers. "Don't ever call yourself that. And getting to know you was *not* a waste of my time. I only wish it could've been on a more honest basis from the beginning." He scooted forward until his knees pressed against hers. "What I feel for you is real."

"What *do* you feel?"

"Way more than I should that erases any professional
line."

"That doesn't tell me much."

He lowered his gaze and clenched his jaw.

"Why did you kiss me back at the tunnel? Was it so
that I would go with you? Because you wanted to inter-
rogate me?"

He shook his head. "No. I kissed you without thinking." He glanced up at her. "I asked you to come with
me because…"

She wrung her hands, desperate for him to say something to mend the broken pieces of her heart. "Because
of what?"

"I didn't want to let you go."

"And lose your asset?"

He slid his palm over both her hands, his warm fingers giving them a slight squeeze. "In that moment, I
didn't see an asset. Only a woman I've fallen for. A
woman who makes me feel things that no one else ever
has. A woman I didn't want to say goodbye to." There
was no filter on his expression. He looked stripped bare.

She wanted to believe him. Truly she did. But he had
told her more lies than she could count. *For months!*

He had used her and maybe he wasn't done yet. It
was possible there was another angle she couldn't see.
How could she trust anything he said until after the full
moon eclipse when he no longer suspected anyone on
the commune of being a domestic terrorist? And even
then, she'd always be wondering what he was hiding,
what he wasn't saying.

She stood and walked around to the other side of the
bed and pulled down the covers. "I'm tired." A bone-

deep weariness was trickling through her, making he
limbs suddenly feel heavy. She glanced at the clock
on the nightstand and couldn't believe how late it was

"I can ask Charlie to stay here with you tonight. I
you'd prefer."

Mercy stiffened at the idea. Did he want to get away
from her now that she had no information to offer? "Did
she know that you were using me this whole time?"

"No. She found out tonight."

That made her feel a little better. About Charlie anyway. "You can call her if it would be easier for you. I
don't want to make you uncomfortable by forcing you
to stay." She climbed into the bed, pulling the covers
up over herself and stared at him.

"I want to be with you, Mercy. I've never wanted
anything more."

There was silence for a long moment that seemed
to grow deeper with each pounding beat of her heart.

His chest heaved as he turned from her. She watched
him clean up the food on the floor and throw away the
trash. He picked up her canvas shoes that were covered
in muck and went into the bathroom.

When he emerged a short while later, carrying her
sneakers, they were spotless.

He set her shoes on the vent of the air-conditioning
unit. Put the chain on the door. Turned out the light.
Trudged to the other bed. Put the holstered gun on the
nightstand and lay down on top of the covers.

She looked at Rocco, who was staring at the ceil-
ing with his hands tucked behind his head, and then at
her shoes again. Cleaning them was a small gesture,

miniuscule in the great scheme of things, but for some reason it touched her deeply.

FOR WHAT SEEMED like hours, Mercy had been tossing and turning. She flopped onto her side. Her gaze slid to the clock. It actually had been hours. Three, to be exact.

She was fatigued, no doubt about that, but she wasn't sure why she couldn't fall asleep.

Maybe it was the foreign environment. The odd smell in the room. The itchy sheets. The mattress that countless others had slept on. The clothes that weren't hers.

Perhaps it was Rocco's betrayal that was like a hot knife in her chest.

Or maybe it was that he was only a couple of feet away, sprawled in a bed, and she wasn't touching him. Her opportunities to do so had been few and far between before and were dwindling with each passing hour.

She had no idea what tomorrow might hold, or even if his feelings for her were genuine. But everything she felt for him and wanted with him was real.

Mercy had spent her entire life worrying about others, their thoughts, their feelings, their expectations, their needs, their wants.

What about her desires?

Why shouldn't she be selfish for once and only think about herself?

No thoughts of the commune. Of her father. Of the ATF. Of the full moon. Of the transgression of sleeping with a nonbeliever.

She wanted to take what she needed on her own terms. This might be her last chance.

Biting her lower lip, she wondered if Rocco was awake. He hadn't moved. He was still on his back, hands clasped behind his head.

She peeled back the covers, slipped out of the bed and climbed onto his.

Propping himself up on his elbows, he looked at her. "What are you doing?"

Slowly, she lowered her head to his, giving him time to pull away. But he didn't. He watched her intently as he leaned in, and then she kissed him. Tentatively. Testing to see if he'd reject her.

Rocco shifted, easing away, and something in her chest sank to her stomach. "What do you want, Mercy?" he asked, his voice soft, almost sweet, as he caressed her cheek.

The words rose in her throat and stuck there.

When she brought Rocco to the compound, she had hoped that he would stay there with her or that she would eventually leave with him, but that they would be together. As a couple. That she would finally feel all the passion and pleasure that she'd only experienced through reading about it in books. *The English Patient. Madame Bovary. Sula. Ulysses. Atonement.*

Although most of them didn't have happy endings. It looked as if her story with Rocco wouldn't either.

But she could make the most of the here and now. "I want you." More than she'd wanted any man she'd ever met.

"Today has been a roller coaster of emotions for you. In a few days, if you still want to, then—"

Mercy pressed her lips to his, silencing him. She didn't know if she'd be able to look at him tomorrow without feeling a rush of anger. Much less in a few days. She didn't know if she'd be in town or on the compound. All she knew for certain was that she had to do everything in her power to protect the commune. From him.

"Tonight," she said. "Unless you don't want this."

Don't want me.

"No, that's not the problem. Rest assured, I want you very much." He sighed. "I just don't want you to do anything you'll regret."

"Too late for that." She pulled her shirt over her head and slipped off the leggings, baring herself to him. "But I want this." She'd fantasized about being with him. So many times. She wondered if her fantasies outnumbered his lies. For now, one outweighed the other. She wouldn't let anger rob her of this joy, this simple pleasure—feeling good in his arms. "My turn to use you."

The words slipped out without thinking, sounding cruel, which wasn't like her.

But he sat up, his gaze raking over her, and gave her a grim smile. "I'm happy to be used by you anytime."

He took her mouth in what began as a simple kiss, but quickly heated when she wrapped her arms around his neck. He lay her down, resting her head on a pillow.

"You're insanely pretty." His words flowed like warm honey over her bruised feelings.

Coming from him, it didn't strike her as a line, but rather a sincere compliment, one that maybe he'd ordinarily be unwilling to give. Still, she reminded herself he wasn't the most honest person.

"The first time I saw you," he said, his breath brushing her lips, "I thought you looked like an angel."

Well, at the moment, she was feeling less than angelic. She spread her legs, opening to him. The solid weight of his body on her was divine. Even better was the feel of the bulge hardening between his thighs.

With one hand, she gripped the back of his neck, the other clutching his shirt. She ached to have him out of his clothes.

As if reading her mind, he pulled off his T-shirt and settled back between her parted legs, that hard bulge resting against her softness. She couldn't stop her hips from rolling against him.

"Turn on the light," she said. "I need to see you." So that she could brand this night on her mind, to warm her in the days ahead.

No matter what happened, no one would be able to take away her memory of this.

He reached over and switched on the lamp. She ran her fingertips through the hair on his chest, over his shoulder, tracing the lines of his tribal tattoo.

God, he's a beautiful one.

The most gorgeous man she'd ever known.

He sucked in a breath when her seeking fingers dipped into his sweatpants and under his boxer briefs. She closed her fingers around the thick, rigid length of him.

"Mercy," he rasped, pulling her hand back. Placing his forearms on either side of her head, he kissed her throat up to her jaw, sending sweet shivers over her skin. "Do you like that?" His voice was huskier with an edge of gravelly heat.

"Yes." Humming, she arched her body, pressing her

breasts against his bare chest, exposing the line of her throat.

His hips jerked, a groan rumbling in his chest. Abruptly, he stopped and leaned over. He unzipped his bag and pulled out a box of condoms, setting them on the nightstand.

She brought his lips back to hers for a hot, steamy rush. Her entire body ached, wanting the contact, the warmth and passion he offered.

"More." Her voice was a rough whisper. "You feel so good. I want to feel you everywhere."

He brushed her mouth with tender kisses, nibbling her jaw, licking her throat, teasing her chest, rolling his tongue around her nipple. On a throaty sigh, she closed her eyes.

"What do you want?" he asked, his breath warm on her breast before closing over her mouth once more.

The deep, thunderous kiss, the roll of his hips, the graze of thick cotton against her soft skin ignited her body so quickly she feared she might burst in a flash of flame.

She spread her hands over his skin, caressing him with a slow reverence that squeezed another guttural groan from him when they came up for air. "I want you. Inside me."

His head popped up. His lips curved wryly. "Tell me what you like?"

"I—I don't know."

Realization flickered in his eyes. "Is this your first time?"

If telling him the truth meant that he'd stop, then she was willing to lie, lie, lie.

"It's important for me to know," he said.

"Yes. But I don't want you to stop."

"I won't. I just…need to slow this down."

While she was ready to rush headlong into it. He body screaming with need that demanded to be ful filled. "I don't want you to go slow."

"Believe me when I say that you do. We need to ex plore a bit. Make sure you enjoy every second. I wan to give you the sweetest pleasure."

Sounded good to her. It was the least he could do "Yes. Please, yes."

He pulled her to him, the kiss primal, absolutely raw and hot.

All her thoughts melted away. There was only him and desire and greed, tangled in her need to have his hands on her. His mouth. *Having* him…any way that she could.

He slipped his hand between her legs, his fingers caressing her, working to open her, and sent her desire soaring. She writhed helplessly, swept up in a wave of wild hunger that overwhelmed her completely, that she had no idea how to satisfy. His strokes were gentle and confident, brushing, teasing over and over at that part of her that was most sensitive.

She turned liquid, molding to the hard contours of his body. Pleasure was an ocean she wanted to drown in. Flooded with breathless sensation and something close to euphoria, she wasn't sure she'd survive it, or if she wanted to. Then he took her even higher, even deeper, at the very same time. The swell built, the pres sure mounting, aching for release. With every breath, every caress, she felt herself, every responsibility, every anchor in her life slipping away. A bittersweet riptide of ecstasy inundated her, reducing her to mindlessness as she came apart in his arms—the first time.

Chapter Eleven

They were a tangle of limbs. All heat and a slow, desperate need that threatened to snap his self-control. He had touched every inch of her exposed skin and she had done likewise, with no hint of shyness. She was a woman on a mission. And he was a man seeking forgiveness with his mouth, his tongue, his fingers, every body part that brought her pleasure.

At last, when he couldn't hold on to his restraint any longer, he gave into his release. She quivered around him again, her nails digging into his back. He groaned at how incredible she felt. Tight, wet, heat. Shuddering, he dropped his face to her neck. Kissed her pulse.

His heart hammered, his breath shallow. Rolling off her, he put his head back on the pillow, drugged with satisfaction. He brought her against his side, nestling her into the crook of his shoulder.

She was perfect. Lean, soft and supple. She'd been so open. So responsive, as if drinking in his touch. Without even trying, she pulled something from him, a tenderness he'd never shown to anyone else. Being with her exceeded his wildest fantasy. Like she'd been made for him.

He'd never made love to anyone like that, feeding off the sight of her in the throes of pleasure, happy to bask in sensation and teeter on the edge. A sweet, terrible form of torture.

Every detail of her pressed close to him struck new chords of desire in him: the lithe lines of her body, the tempting curve of her breasts, the sunny blond hair that spilled over his chest, catching the light like liquid gold. And most of all, her beautiful face.

Before he'd fully caught his breath, she disentangled herself from him, slipped out of bed and padded toward the bathroom. Every movement was graceful and careful like a cat finding her way across slippery, uneven ground.

The door closed. The toilet flushed. Water ran.

He discarded the used condom in the trash bin, double-checked the chain on the door and crawled into bed.

Minutes later, she came out, but didn't meet his eyes. She climbed into the other bed, switched off the lamp and turned her back to him.

An odd pressure churned in his chest.

"Mercy..." His voice failed him, his brain staggering at his inability to come up with the right words. He thought she'd get back into bed with him. That she'd want to be held. Or talk. "Are you sore?" he asked in concern, remembering how delicate she was, how tight. He'd done his best to tamp down his urges and go slowly, gently, so as not to cause her any pain. "Mercy, are you okay?"

"Thank you for giving me what I wanted."

To be thanked felt odd. *Wrong.*

He waited for her to say more. When she didn't, he assumed it was because she was still upset with him despite what had just transpired between them. With a hot stab in the pit of his stomach, he said, "I'm sorry I didn't trust you with the truth sooner. I never meant to hurt you. If I could go back and handle it differently, I would."

But then he realized that if he had told her he was an ATF agent that night in USD, after her panic attack, he still would've driven her away.

"I'm tired," she said. "Good night."

The knot behind his sternum tightened and spread. Tendrils of anxiety coiled through him like choking vines.

He'd never be able to separate the months of lies from all the moments of honesty.

As a consequence, he feared losing her for good.

WHEN ROCCO AWAKENED the next morning, he was unsure of the time, a rarity for him. The situation didn't look any better in the light of day. If anything, things were worse.

They got ready in silence. She wasn't being modest, not hiding her body, but they had moved around each other, with her going to great pains to avoid any physical contact. He took her cue and kept his distance.

Not knowing how long they might need the room he didn't check out. They climbed into Charlie's muscle car. He brought the engine roaring to life. "We can stop and grab breakfast," he suggested as he pulled out of the lot.

With her arms crossed, she stared out the window. "I'm not hungry."

"Then we can get some coffee at a café and talk."

"Before you hand me off to my next babysitter?"

He swallowed a sigh. At least she was talking to him. "Do you want to discuss what happened last night?"

"We had sex. What else is there to say?"

It had been more than that for him, and he'd suspected, with it being her first time, that it had been more to her as well. "How you're feeling for starters?"

"Angry. Betrayed. Confused." She shifted in her seat. "Satisfied?"

Not even close.

"Where are we going?" she asked.

"To task force headquarters. Really, it's just office space on Second Street. I have to meet with my boss, and another agent, one with the FBI, Becca Hammond, will want to speak with you."

Her eyes grew wide. "Why?"

"It's standard procedure. There's nothing for you to worry about."

Frown lines bracketed her mouth. "If I'm going to be interrogated again, this time by a stranger, I'd rather go someplace familiar. Like the Underground Self-Defense school."

He shook his head. "It would be safer and more convenient to take you to headquarters. And you won't be interrogated. Only questioned."

"Am I under arrest?"

"No, of course not."

"Then if you want me to speak with your FBI friend,

we'll do it on my terms, at the USD. Or we won't do it at all."

He didn't like it, but he'd already put her through so much. Allowing her to choose the location where she'd speak with Becca was a small request. There were no windows in the office at USD. If she was in there with the door closed, then she'd be kept out of sight, mitigating any issues. "Okay. USD it is."

More uneasy silence settled between them, and he hated it. "You must have questions. About me. About my job."

Her gaze met his, those blue eyes piercing him. "Is Rocco Sharp even your real name?"

"Yes and no. It's Rocco Kekoa. Sharp is my mother's maiden name. I started using it as part of my cover when I was assigned to the task force."

"Your time in the military and special ops?"

"All true. Enlisted in the army at eighteen. Served for ten years, including two tours in Afghanistan and a spec op mission in Syria."

"What about your childhood, growing up with Charlie on a ranch in Hawaii, wrangling longhorn cattle?"

"Those are some of my fondest memories." He came from a long line of paniolos, or Hawaiian cowboys. "When work slows down for me, I'm going to fix up my ranch here and get some horses just like I told you."

"The story about falling out of a tree and breaking your arm? The fights you got into with bullies?"

He knew he deserved her suspicion and welcomed her questions, but it didn't make it any easier.

"It really happened." He'd shared things with her that

he'd never told anyone else. Had spilled the stories that made him who he was in their first few days together and he wasn't sure why. It hadn't been done as a maneuver to manipulate her. Maybe it was how she made him feel…at ease, like it was safe to be himself. She had such a generous heart. Maybe that was it.

She stilled his usually restless mind. Filled the spaces he hadn't known were empty with warmth and light.

Whatever it was, he wanted more. He wanted her. So much so that he'd do whatever was necessary to rebuild her trust. Prove how deeply he felt for her.

"I enjoyed our time together at USD. Looked forward to it. You have to believe me when I tell you that I care about you." Regardless of his job, after her panic attack, he wouldn't have let her go back to the compound alone. He recognized it as her survival instinct kicking in, a sign she needed help, even if she didn't realize it.

"How long have you been watching us?" she asked, ignoring him.

"The task force stood up a little over a year ago."

"Why *us*?"

There were multiple factors, but he'd give her the main ones. "Your numbers have grown really fast. Along with your stockpile of weapons. Your father has successfully converted over five hundred people, more than half that number in the last four years, convincing them to change their names, to hand over their possessions and to live in a secluded, heavily armed compound." The Shining Light had amassed nearly two thousand weapons, including automatic and assault rifles, shotguns, revolvers, and his task force had reports of grenades and other explosives, though Rocco hadn't

seen those. Still, Marshall McCoy had a small army a
his disposal. "It's a disaster waiting to happen."

She inhaled a shaky breath and shook her head. "Yo
still think my commune is a threat?"

"I think your father is. He's a dangerous man, wield
ing a lot of power," he said, and she stiffened as she
looked away from him. He was only sending her de
fenses into overdrive. He needed to tread carefully. "
have seen the good things happening on the compound
How happy everyone appears. How much they love
being on the compound. How you look out for one an
other."

"Like any decent community should." She bit her
lower lip. "If you were able to find the weapons supplier and prevent whatever tragedy is supposed to happen tomorrow, would your task force leave us alone?"

His brain stuck on her use of *your* and *us*. Neither
was a good sign. "Do you know something?"

"No. I was just wondering if it's worth it for you to
risk your life by messing with the Devil's Warriors."

Risking his life by infiltrating such groups was his
job, but he didn't think telling her that would improve
things.

He pulled into the lot behind USD and parked. "I'll
do whatever is necessary to stop the illegal shipment of
weapons across state lines and save lives."

She fixed him with a stare. "Does that include telling me more lies?"

Shutting off the engine, he turned in his seat, facing
her. "I will never lie to you again."

She narrowed her eyes and chewed on her lip. "You

didn't answer my question. If you got what you needed, would you leave the Shining Light alone?"

"It's not my call to make," he said, and she grimaced. "But what I can tell you is that I didn't see anything to justify a warrant." If he had found explosives, or if they had assaulted him, drugged him or used ayahuasca outside of religious purposes, then that would have been a different story. "Any cooperation from the Shining Light would go a long way to establishing goodwill with law enforcement."

"I could speak to my father."

That was a horrible idea.

Mercy was a direct threat to her father's autocratic power. After she helped Rocco escape, Marshall would do anything to bring his daughter to heel.

"You're out. I don't think you should see or talk to anyone from the commune until you're sure about what you want to do."

She'd gotten a taste of true freedom. Once he and Charlie spoon-fed her more, showed Mercy the community they had forged, where they also took care of each other, she wouldn't want to go back.

He was certain of it.

Lowering her head, unease moved across her face.

"Do you believe I care about you?" he asked. "That my feelings are real?"

She shrugged.

How could he convince her? "What would it take?"

"Time. Seeing proof through your actions."

"Then, *please*, give me time. I'm begging you." And he was not the kind of man who *ever* begged. He peered closer, trying to draw her gaze to his, but she wouldn't

look at him. He wanted to hug her, hold her, make lov
to her until she forgave him. But he didn't dare touc
her. "Will you?"

ALL MERCY COULD tell him was the truth. "I don't know.

He looked out the window at the back door to USD

He glanced over at her. "Come on." They got out o
the car. "Listen to Brian. Do whatever he asks. He'l
keep you safe while I'm gone."

"Don't tell me that he's a part of your task force, too,"
she said, half-joking.

"Actually, he is. But he's Laramie PD. It's because
of the task force that we became such good friends."

For some reason, those facts made her even more
uneasy.

Rocco fiddled with the keys and unlocked the back
door. After they stepped inside, he turned the bolt, locking it behind them. They walked down a corridor, passing the bathroom and entered the main front space.

Charlie was in the middle of teaching a class. Brian
stood off to the side with his hands clasped. An LPD
cruiser was parked out front.

When Brian spotted them, he came over. "Good
morning. Why don't we talk in the office?" He led the
way.

They stepped inside and Rocco shut the door.

"Anything?" Brian asked.

"Afraid not. I'm going to update Nash, and I gave
Mercy a heads-up about Becca."

With a grim look, Brian nodded.

"Good idea to have a couple of uniforms posted out
front," Rocco said.

"The visual makes a nice deterrent."

"My father wouldn't send anyone after me," Mercy said. "It's a waste of resources."

"Would you give us a minute?" Rocco asked Brian, and his friend left them alone in the office. "You underestimate your dad. He'd do anything to keep you under his yoke."

"He wouldn't kidnap me and drag me back. I'm not an escaped prisoner." Although she felt like one.

"No, he'd only manipulate you into a courtship with a man you don't want, in front of your entire commune. And that's after years of his machinations to prevent you from claiming *penumbroyage*. But you really think he's above sending Alex or someone else to haul you back?"

"Yes." She tried to picture it. Bound and gagged and tossed into a vehicle like a hostage. Her father's methods were never so crude. He operated with far more finesse.

Over the years, whenever he'd gotten her to fall into line, he'd always managed to make her feel as if it was her own choice. She saw him clearly, for what he was. A master puppeteer, pulling everyone's strings.

Maybe the immense power of being a prophet had corrupted him.

That little voice in her head whispered to her. *The Light can illuminate. But it can also blind.*

She still believed in the commune and always would. But she was ready for a change. To choose her own path. To get out from under her father's thumb.

To be free.

"I hope you're right and those officers parked outside turn out to be a waste of resources," Rocco said.

"You don't need to worry about me. You should

worry about yourself if you're still planning to go to the Devil's Warriors."

"The odds are high that they use the same weapons supplier as the Shining Light. It's our best bet at this point."

It would take time to track down the supplier and once Rocco did—if that gang hadn't hurt or killed him—it would be too late. The full moon was tomorrow.

She didn't think her father was a terrorist, but she also couldn't dismiss an informant directly linking him to whatever was going to happen.

"I may be angry enough to strangle you, but I don't want anything bad to happen to you."

"Oh, I see, you want the pleasure of doing it yourself." His mouth hitched in a sexy grin. "How about when you're in the mood to *use* me again, I let you tie me down so you can have your way with me."

She couldn't believe he was making a joke at a time like this.

His eyes trailed from her face down over her body. His gaze was like a caress, her skin igniting as if it were his fingers doing the work. Awareness sizzled between them, almost as if a fuse had been lit in the silence.

Yet, he made no move to touch her. He hadn't all morning, which she realized was because she'd given him the cold shoulder. Nonetheless, it irritated her.

As absurd as it sounded, she wanted to be so irresistible to him that he had no choice but to touch her.

"I never said there'd be a next time."

His grin fell, his eyes sobering. "I don't deserve you, Mercy McCoy. You're too good for me." He cupped her arm, his grip gentle and firm, as he leaned over and kissed her forehead. "But if you don't give me a chance to show you what you mean to me, I'll regret it until the day I die."

He enveloped her in a gentle hug. Everything about it had her struggling to ignore her bone-deep awareness of him. The feel of his powerful body against hers. The delicious, masculine scent of him. How safe and protected his embrace made her feel.

How right it felt, even though her mind screamed that it was wrong.

Then he let her go and left.

Closing her eyes, she took a steady breath, trying to push aside her complex and unsettling feelings for him. She couldn't afford to be fooled again. But despite telling herself not to believe him, she did. He'd spoken so fervently, as though the words had been from the heart.

It could've been an act. He could be playing you again.

Deep down, she wanted Rocco to be the man she'd thought he was.

Even though last night had been her first time, the depths of affection and consideration he'd showered on her exceeded lust.

He hadn't had sex with her. He'd made love to her. With every kiss, every touch, she'd felt cherished. Their bodies had reflected everything given, everything shared as they had joined as one. She'd felt his strength and gentleness, for a moment, possibly even his soul.

And that made his betrayal sting like acid, below the skin, down to her blood.

Getting close to her had been his duty. His assignment.

Which reminded her that she had a duty as well. To the commune and all the innocent people who called it home.

Brian came into the office, pulling her from her thoughts, and she knew what she had to do next with staggering clarity.

"Can I get you anything?" he asked. "Coffee? Tea? A magazine?"

"We didn't eat breakfast. Would you mind getting me something from Delgado's?"

"Sure. Do you know what you want?"

"Anything vegetarian." Not that she was hungry.

"They've got tasty breakfast burritos. Eggs, beans, avocado—"

"Sounds perfect."

He picked up the phone and placed the order. "It'll take twenty minutes. Since it's under their delivery minimum, I'll run down the block to pick it up when it's ready."

"Thank you. And you know what, I will take a magazine on second thought."

Brian grabbed a stack from the table near the entrance and set it down on the desk in the office. They all dealt with fitness.

"Is it okay if I had some time to myself, to process my thoughts? Everything that Rocco told me is still quite a shock."

"Of course. I won't disturb you until I've got your breakfast." He went to the threshold and stopped. "When you're feeling up to it, Charlie wants to talk to you about your options here in town. No pressure or anything. Rocco isn't the only one here for you. Charlie, me and others you haven't met yet will help you make a transition. We just want you to know that you're not alone."

After everything, somehow that was the thing to bring her closest to tears.

"Thank you."

He left the office, shutting the door behind him.

Mercy sat down at the desk, found a notepad and pen. She wrote a quick note to explain her decision to Rocco.

Looking it over, she knew the words wouldn't be enough, but it was the best she could do. Then she picked up the phone and dialed the number to her father's office.

The line rang and rang. She prayed she wouldn't have to call Alex to reach him.

On the sixth ring, her father answered, "Hello."

"It's me. Mercy."

Silence. Deliberate. Calculated, surely.

"I knew you'd call," he said. "I foresaw it. Are you hurt?"

"I'm fine."

"That's not true. I can hear it in your voice. Your heart is hurting."

This was what he did, each and every time. Crawled inside her head.

Had he foreseen this? Could he hear it? Her pain, her confusion, her concern.

"I need someone to pick me up." They both knew who that someone would be. She almost asked that it *not* be Alex, but he wouldn't send anyone else and that might work to her advantage.

"Certainly, my dear."

"It has to be in less than twenty minutes. The parking lot behind USD."

"As you wish."

She hung up the phone and glanced at the clock on the wall.

Heart hammering in her chest, she jumped to her feet, hurried to the door and cracked it open. She peeked out.

The hour-long self-defense class was still going on and would continue for almost another half hour. Brian stood near the front door like a sentinel, his head on a swivel as though he was scanning the street.

She moved back and sat where she could see through the slight opening in the door. Thumbing through a magazine, she kept an eye on the time and on Brian.

Sweat trickled down her spine. Her thoughts spun. Was this a mistake?

She shook off the doubt and ignored her jittering nerves. This was the only way. If her gamble didn't work, then the commune would remain under the scrutiny of law enforcement. The Shining Light would be blamed if something horrible happened tomorrow.

And Rocco…

He could be hurt.

This was a calculated risk. The stakes were too high not to take it.

Brian grabbed his cowboy hat and placed it on his head. He gestured something to Charlie. She nodded in response. Once he pushed through the front door, Mercy was on her feet.

She sucked in a deep breath. Made sure the note was

in the center of the desk, where it would be easily seen. Hustled to the door.

Crossing the main workout area, she caught Charlie's eye and mouthed *bathroom*. Through the front window she watched Brian say something to the police officers in the squad car before he headed down the street.

Mercy turned down the hall. Stealing a furtive glance over her shoulder, she passed the bathroom. No one was behind her. She ran to the back door, flipped the latch on the bolt and shoved outside.

Alex sat behind the wheel of a black SUV, waiting for her. She scurried to the rear door and grabbed the handle, but it was locked.

He lowered the window. "Sit up front with me," he said, cocking his arm on the back of the seat, staring at her. "The rules have changed."

Anger whipped through her, hot as a lash, but she pushed it aside. She needed to focus on her objective and not let anything sidetrack her from achieving it.

She hopped into the front seat. Before she closed the door, he sped off. He turned onto the side street, Garfield. At the stop sign, he made a right on the main road, Third Street.

He glanced down at the jeans that she wore, but he didn't comment on them. Not that he needed to. The twist of his mouth and narrowing of his eyes told her plenty. He drove right past USD and the patrol car.

She gave one last look at Charlie instructing the class.

"Yesterday, Empyrean told me that you'd be back," he said. "But for the first time in my life, I doubted him."

She looked at Alex, her gaze falling to his Shining Light tattoo at the base of his throat. He had always been a true believer. Devout to the core.

"Is there something planned for tomorrow?" she asked.

"The shedding ceremony. You know that."

Out the window, she spotted Brian leaving Delgado's, holding the breakfast that she would never eat. She didn't bother ducking down. They were gone too quickly, heading out of downtown.

"No, something else that's been kept quiet," she said, hoping to learn what she needed to from him, sparing her from dealing with her father.

All he had to do was fill in the missing pieces to Rocco's puzzle for her. Then she was prepared to open the door and jump from a moving vehicle to avoid going back.

Alex raised an eyebrow. "Like what?"

"Something awful. Something violent."

He gave her a questioning glance and she saw it in his eyes. He had no clue what she was talking about. She could always read him like an open book.

"My father is grooming you to succeed him. He shares a lot with you."

"Because he trusts me."

Which in turn meant she wasn't fully trusted. It was the only explanation as to why she was kept in the dark.

She reached over and put her hand on his forearm. He glanced down at the point of contact.

"You're happy that I'm coming back, aren't you?"

"Of course." His mouth lifted in a bright smile that shone through his eyes.

"Do you want to make me happy?"

"Yes. Any good husband wants to please his wife."

Her stomach twisted at messing with his emotions. "I want you to tell me who supplies us with weapons."

"What?" He stiffened.

"Just give me a name."

He stared at her, the cloud of disbelief lifting from his face, and snatched his arm away. "You're asking me this because of *him*. Aren't you?" He barked a vicious laugh. "Even if I knew, I wouldn't tell you after the stunt you pulled yesterday." Swerving off the road onto the shoulder, he slammed on the brakes and threw the car into Park. He turned and glared at her. "You've never taken my affection for you seriously. But you need to because I'd rather see you dead than living in darkness with that man." His eyes burned with a fury she'd never seen in him before. "Do you understand me?"

She swallowed around the cold lump of fear in her throat. "I understand."

All too well. She was never going to marry Alex, so when it came to his *love* for her, it boiled down to kill or be killed.

But he was a problem that had to wait.

Pulling off with squealing tires, Alex hit the gas pedal, racing toward the compound.

Her heart sank.

If her father had trusted anyone with the name of the arms dealer and details about any heinous event that he was either aware of or had in the works, then it would've been Alex.

That left her with no other choice.

She had to return to the compound and ask her father for help. He would give it after a performance full of melodrama designed to saddle her with guilt. But it would come at a heavy price that she'd have to pay.

Chapter Twelve

Seated at the conference table across from Nash and Becca, Rocco was going through his debriefing when his cell phone rang. This was hard enough without interruptions. Not looking to see who it was, he silenced the phone.

He took a breath, collecting his thoughts, chiding himself for his failure. "As I was saying—"

Nash's phone rang. Sighing, he took it out of his pocket. "It's Brian."

A cold fist gripped Rocco's gut. *Mercy.* "Put him on speaker."

Nash answered, "I'm here with Rocco and Becca. We're all on the line. What's up?"

"Mercy is gone."

Shoving up out of his chair, Rocco stood and pressed his palms to the solid wood table. "What do you mean? How is that possible?"

"I went to get her something to eat," Brian said. "While I was gone, she left."

Rocco struggled to understand. "You mean she was taken?"

"No." Brian sighed. "She walked out the back door."

Rocco blinked and the room spun.

"Any idea why she would leave?" Nash asked Brian. "Did something happen?"

"She left a note."

"Read it," Rocco snapped more harshly than he'd intended.

"'Dear Rocco, my father is the only one who can give you the answers you need in time. Stay away from the Devil's Warriors. Please trust me.'"

The words hit him like a sucker punch. Her questions about whether the task force would leave the Shining Light alone if they got what they needed suddenly made sense. She'd been planning to take off for the compound before he'd even left her at USD.

"If she's on foot," Rocco said, "you can catch her."

"I drove around in a five-block radius. No sign of her. I'm sure she got a ride."

Swearing under his breath, Rocco grabbed his phone and headed for the door.

"Wait," Becca said, stopping him. "She asked you to trust her. Running off to the compound and making a scene would be doing the exact opposite. Maybe you should let this play out. We can still use the time for alternative plans."

"To hell with that."

"Becca is right," Nash said. "She's already gone. Give her a chance to work on her father. If you haven't heard from her in a couple of hours, then we'll all go together. It won't take long to get to her."

MERCY PADDED INTO her father's office.

He got up from his chair. His gaze raked over her,

lingering on her jeans, but he said nothing about her clothing. He came around and greeted her with a tight hug. "Oh, my dear child. Praise the Light for your return." He ushered her to the sofa by the windows. "Alex, leave us."

"Sir, I need to tell you—"

Her father waved him off. "It can wait. Mercy's well-being must come first."

"But, Empyrean—"

"Silence." Her father's tone sharpened, but he didn't raise his voice. "Her eternal soul hangs in the balance. Nothing you have to say is more important." He tsk-tsked him away as if Alex was a dog.

But that was how he treated them both, like pets.

Alex closed the door to the office behind him.

Her father guided her down onto the sofa and sat beside her. She clasped her hands in her lap, unsure of how to proceed.

He didn't ask any questions. Didn't goad. Didn't chastise. Didn't push. He simply put a big, warm palm over her folded hands. Staring at her, he remained silent, his gaze soft, his demeanor calm.

There was no atmosphere of pressure. If anything, his approach conveyed support. Love. He was the picture of a nurturing father.

Or the perfect predator laying a trap.

The silence grew, expanding, sucking up the air in the room until she couldn't breathe.

"I need your help," she finally said.

He nodded as though he'd expected the words. "I'm listening."

There were two ways she could play this. One was

to be coy, to filter details, to break down in fake tears, asking for forgiveness.

But Empyrean was much better at this game.

So she went with the second option. The unvarnished truth.

She spilled her guts about everything—Rocco using her, that he was an ATF agent, the task force investigating the Shining Light, needing the name of the weapons supplier, the dead informant in Rocco's arms, his last words about an act of domestic terrorism planned for tomorrow, that the commune would be scapegoats, that their community would suffer, that she would give anything to protect them and Rocco.

"Rocco is going to try to get information from the Devil's Warriors, but he's going to get hurt. Please. We have to stop this. Right now. Before it's too late."

Her father wasn't quick to respond. But when he finally opened his mouth, he asked, "Did you sleep with him?"

She hesitated, but he'd know if she lied. "Yes."

Another slow nod. The look on his face was almost one of relief. "Sometimes an itch needs to be scratched. Not knowing can be more powerful than the act itself. Our imaginations are so fantastical, running wild, filling in the blanks, over and over, in such colorful, lurid ways. While memories, ah, those are designed to fade. In time."

Her stomach clenched. "Out of everything I just told you, that's what you're focused on?"

His grip on her hands tightened. "Do you want to know why I could never pick you to succeed me to lead the commune?"

A dangerous question. But one she needed answered or she'd wonder for the rest of her life, with her imagination filling in the blanks. "Yes."

"When your mother left us, it was like you had one foot planted here, and one foot always reaching for the outside world as if to follow her. You questioned everything. Questioned me. Stopped truly believing. Her last words to you were 'the light can illuminate. But it can also blind.' And after that you never looked at me the same way. With reverence in your eyes."

Mercy's heart practically stopped. For years, she'd thought her mother had died. She didn't have memories of her anymore. There were no pictures of her anywhere. She couldn't even remember what she looked like.

The little voice in her head, warning her, was her mother's.

"My mother left? Why? Is she still alive?" A flurry of questions stormed through her mind.

"Out of everything you told me, that's what you're focused on?" he asked, regurgitating her words, making her feel sick. "I thought time was of the essence to help Rocco. Would you prefer to talk about your mother instead?"

Mercy gritted her teeth, hating this game. Because he was so much better at it than she was.

MARSHALL KNEW WHAT his daughter's response would be, what she would choose. Or rather who.

Certainly not the mother she barely remembered.

All this time he thought Rocco was the problem when really, he was the solution to one. Marshall was at his wit's end about how to get Mercy to abandon her desire to leave and accept her role in the commune. There had been times when he'd gotten close to forcing her to take her vows to shed her former self and receive the tattoo. But he never did out of fear. A cold, stark fear that she might still leave. And if she did, after taking her vows, then he could never allow her to return. She would be considered forever lost to them. One of the *fallen*.

But now she would make the sacrifice of her own free will.

Thanks to a nonbeliever.

Once this was all said and done, he'd have to send Rocco a gift basket with some of their finest goods: produce, homemade soap and a jar of their lavender honey.

"In helping Rocco, we help the Shining Light," she said, and he couldn't tell if she was trying to convince him or herself. "We have to protect the commune. They're coming for us."

Hardly breaking news. "They've been coming for a while. They planted an informant in here."

Shock spilled across her face. "Do you know who?"

He gave her a knowing smile. "Sophia."

Mercy flinched. "You've known this whole time?"

"It's the reason I started sleeping with her. As soon as I did and she saw what her life could be, she told me everything. Confessed in my bed. Her handler was Becca Hammond. I had Sophia sever all contact and she did. I'm not surprised that they would stoop so low as to seduce you next, treating you like a tawdry pawn. They would cross any line, trample on hearts, tell any lie to achieve their aims."

She looked like she was going to retch.

"Can I get you a glass of water?" he asked.

Taking a deep breath, she shook her head.

"Do you still want to protect Rocco?"

Mercy lowered her eyes.

Out of shame, no doubt. The poor girl did want to protect him. Still.

What a disappointment.

"The only way to protect the commune," she said, "is to give his task force the name of our weapons supplier and help them stop whatever is planned for tomorrow. Do you know anything about that?"

"I *am* the prophet." He didn't know what was planned, but he did know who was planning the event. It would be big. Loud. And violent. In the end, the chaos and tragedy would increase their numbers. But first he had to protect and preserve what he already had. "I can be of service to this task force. But I need something from you first."

She grew still as stone. "What?"

The flames of rebellion had burned in her for far too long. The time had come for him to extinguish that fire.

"If I do this—if I help Rocco without delay—then you must agree to take your vows to the community and seal your union with Alex on a date of my choosing."

Mercy paled, all the blood draining from her lovely face. If only she could see that this was for her own good. Once she married Alex and had a child the rest would fall into place.

"The Light has spoken through me. What say you?" he asked.

Tears welled in her bright blue eyes that were the same as her mother's.

But he would take his daughter's sorrow and turn it into joy, like water into wine.

"Okay," she said.

He reined in his impatience. "I need to hear the words, Mercy."

"So shall it be."

Chapter Thirteen

"I demand to see Mercy McCoy," Rocco said to the guard at the front gate. "I'm not leaving until I do."

Nash flashed his badge. "Special Agent Garner and this is Special Agent Hammond," he said, gesturing to her in the back seat. "None of us are leaving until we know Ms. McCoy is all right."

The guy stepped into the guardhouse, picked up the phone and made a call. He turned his back to them as he spoke on the phone. A minute later he opened the gate and came back up to Nash's car. "You're all free to go."

Nash drove up the hill to Light House, which glittered and sparkled in the sunlight. A beautiful facade hiding all of Marshall McCoy's ugly secrets.

Armed guards met them as they parked.

Getting out of the truck, Rocco noticed that his Bronco had been pulled up near the front of the house. Like they had been expecting him.

"You can go on up," Shawn said.

They ascended the steps to the front door, where Alex was waiting with a big, goading smile that made Rocco ache to punch him in the face.

"Empyrean is eager to speak with you." Alex opened the door, letting them in. "Please remove your shoes."

Rocco was already doing so in the foyer. Nash looked uncertain, but he complied as did Becca.

Alex led the way to the office with his hand on the hilt of his gun holstered on his hip.

The door was wide-open.

Mercy was inside, sitting on a sofa in the back of the office. She looked up, a grim expression on her face as she met his gaze with solemn eyes, but she didn't get up when they entered the room.

"Welcome." Marshall approached them with his arms open in greeting. "I'm Empyrean."

"Special Agent Nash Garner."

"Special Agent Becca Hammond."

Recognition flashed in Marshall's eyes. "I've been looking forward to meeting you, Agent Hammond. Your reputation precedes you."

Becca schooled her features, not giving anything away with her face, but she put a protective hand on her belly that spoke volumes.

"Please have a seat." Marshall gestured to the chairs.

"I'll stand," Rocco said, and Alex came up alongside him. He glanced at Mercy again, wondering if she was okay, but she lowered her head.

Nash and Becca took seats in the chairs that faced the desk where Marshall sat.

"My daughter has relayed troubling things to me. I'm glad you're all here so that we can clear things up. It's my understanding that you, Agent Kekoa, had an informant give you a disturbing message before dying in your arms. Is that correct?"

Had Mercy told him everything?

"Yes, that's correct."

"Would you mind repeating that exact message for all of us?" Marshall asked. "For the sake of clarity so that we might be on the same page."

"He said that on September nineteenth something big, something horrible was going to happen and that McCoy had planned it all."

"Ah." Marshall tipped his back as though struck with a revelation. "Naturally, you assumed your informant was referring to me."

Rocco's blood turned to ice. "Yes, he was spying on you."

"May I venture to guess that your informant was Dr. Percy Tiggs? I read about his passing in the news. His son is one of my flock and Dr. Tiggs didn't exactly celebrate the fact."

Nash threw Rocco a furtive glance, but none of them responded.

"I understand if you're not permitted to confirm or deny," Marshall said. "But I believe your informant was talking about my brother, Cormac. The other *lesser* known McCoy."

Mercy's head popped up, her eyes snapping wide in shock. She stared at her father before glancing at Rocco. She shook her head, and he could tell that she didn't know.

Was it possible that Percy had been talking about Marshall's brother?

"Dr. Tiggs regularly went to his camp to tend to their horses. Mac was too radical for the Shining Light. Dangerous in the extremism that he preached—

antigovernment and no laws but those of Mother Nature. He eventually left with a bunch of my people, our people, since we started this together. His faction broke away nineteen years ago, on the same day that my wife, Ayanna, left. Three paths that had been one became fractured and diverged."

Mercy stiffened and wrung her hands.

There was something more at play here, between her and her father. What sick game was he up to?

"I don't consider Mac one of the fallen, not like my former wife," Marshall said. "He calls his people the Brotherhood of the Silver Light, but they venture far too close to the sun. Whereas Ayanna wandered off in darkness. But if something big and horrible is planned for tomorrow, Mac would be the McCoy that you're looking for."

Had Percy meant that they had been wrong about Marshall? Had he been trying to tell him about Mac McCoy?

"What about your weapons supplier?" Rocco asked.

"I make all my arrangements through Mac. Like I said, he's not fallen. Contact is permitted."

"Where can we find him?" Nash asked.

"Up in the mountains. But he has a tight-knit group. Not so easily infiltrated like mine," Marshall said, sliding a glance at Becca. "You won't get access or answers without my assistance."

Becca leaned forward, crossing her legs at the ankles. "What would getting your assistance require?"

"I feel certain that my cooperation would go a long, long way in fostering goodwill with your task force." Marshall smiled at Rocco.

Those were his words verbatim. Mercy had told him everything.

"But I would like verbal assurances," Marshall added, "that we will no longer be harassed or spied on and that I can in good faith tell my people that they have nothing to fear from you."

"So long as you don't break the law," Nash said, "you'll have nothing to worry about. And yes, your unsolicited cooperation will not only be significant, but also documented. Which will carry weight."

Marshall clasped his hands on the desk. "This is how we'll proceed. I'll send Rocco to Cormac's camp. Along with Mercy."

Alex made a guttural noise like that of a wounded animal, drawing everyone's attention. "No, you can't."

"Silence." Marshall raised his palm at Alex. "It's the only way Mac will let Rocco in. If she's there with him, pretending to be his betrothed, and explains that he's too radical for my people, there won't be questions. Then it will be up to Agent Kekoa to do his job."

"No!" Alex stormed up to the desk. "You can't do this!"

"You forget yourself, son." Marshall stood and put a hand on his shoulder. "Have faith in me. All will be well. Mercy has decided to take her vows to the Shining Light and to marry you. Isn't that right, my dear?"

Everyone turned to look at her. Rocco's heart throbbed in his chest.

Biting her lip, she held his stare. "Yes."

His lungs squeezed so hard he could barely breathe.

"See." Marshall patted Alex on the back. "This trip to the mountains will help the task force stop something heinous from happening and allow Mercy to say her goodbyes. I have things well in hand."

Alex remained silent, but he didn't look convinced.

"Won't Cormac question the timing of their arrival and think it suspicious?" Nash asked.

Nodding, Marshall sat back down. "Certainly. That's why it has to be Mercy who accompanies him. Mac never could deny her anything."

"But that was when I was five." Mercy got up, wrapping her arms around herself, and strode to the window. "I don't even remember him."

"Doesn't matter." Her father leaned back in his chair. "He'll remember you and he will let you into his camp. I've foreseen it."

"We appreciate your cooperation." Becca shifted in her chair like she was uncomfortable. "But why would you give up your brother?"

"There is no love lost between me and Mac. He's always had a taste for violence. Giving him up to protect my people and other innocent lives is the only prudent choice. Wouldn't you agree?"

"It would appear so," Becca said.

"When would you send them?" Nash asked.

"Shortly. It's a two-hour drive. I'd want them there before it gets dark. Is this agreeable to you?"

Nash stood. "Yes, yes, it is."

"One last thing," Marshall said. "I should warn you that sending backup to the area for Rocco would not be advisable. My brother keeps men in the woods and on the mountain on constant patrol. They'll spot other agents creeping around and then there's no telling what will happen. For this to work, it has to be Mercy and Rocco on their own."

"Thank you for your cooperation." Nash shook Marshall's hand. "Rocco, a moment in the hall."

Rocco stepped out of the office along with Nash and Becca as Alex began protesting this arrangement again.

"I don't like it," Becca said, once they were out of earshot.

Nash nodded in agreement. "Neither do I."

"What choice do we have?" Rocco folded his arms, flicking a glance back at the office.

Mercy stayed near the window, her face pallid, her gaze focused on him and not Alex, who was ranting.

"You won't have any backup if something goes wrong," Nash said.

That didn't worry him. "I'm used to working on my own. It's the nature of the undercover beast."

"Her father is playing a dangerous game," Becca said. "With his daughter right at the center of it all. That's what bothers me. It doesn't fit with his profile, endangering her. I feel like we're missing something here."

Rocco felt likewise. "I've got to be honest with you, Nash. Under normal circumstances, the mission would come first. No matter what. But keeping Mercy safe will be a priority." All his concern was for her.

"What if Marshall calls his brother and lets him know what's up? This could be a setup," Becca said.

"It could be," Rocco agreed, "but we don't have much choice. Time is running out and this is our best option."

"Find out what you can," Nash said, "then get out of there with her. Don't try to be a hero by stopping whatever they have planned on your own. Just relay the in-formation in time and we'll do the rest."

"Roger that." He couldn't afford to take the chance of heroics. Not with Mercy's life on the line. "Becca, would you mind driving my car back into town? We'll take one of McCoy's vehicles up into the mountains."

"Sure. No problem."

"The keys should be in the car. If not, one of the guards will be able to get them for you."

"Safe travels," she said.

Nash and Becca headed out.

Staring at the scene in the office, resolve hardened inside him like steel. He was going to do everything in his power to protect her, from her father, from Alex, from her uncle. From any threat.

He strode inside, and Alex's head whipped toward him, his eyes filled with hatred.

"Enough." Marshall pressed his palm to the man's chest. "You must trust me in this." He drew a deep breath. "Mercy, you're still looking quite pale. Are you well?"

"Low blood sugar. We didn't have breakfast."

"I don't think it best for you two to linger until the commune gathers for lunch, which won't be for another hour. The more time you have at Mac's camp, Rocco, the better," Marshall said, almost sounding helpful. "But it's a long drive. Let the four of us break bread together in peace before you go."

"An early lunch would be good," Mercy said in a defeated way, as if all the fight had been kicked out of her. "If that's okay with you?" She looked at Rocco.

"I'm starving." He'd prefer not to endure an awkward

meal with the mighty Empyrean and jealous Alex, but he could eat. "And we still need to know where we're going and what to expect once we get there."

"Alex, go to the kitchen. See what the cooks can rustle up for us quickly." Marshall shooed him out, and Alex stalked off with clenched fists.

Rocco hoped that guy wasn't petty enough to spit in his food.

Mercy's father stepped around behind his desk, unlocked the top drawer and pulled out a map. "Here, let me show you what roads to take."

Marshall pointed out the route that ran right through the mountains, past the overlook where he was supposed to meet Percy. It was possible that the doctor might have been fleeing from Cormac's camp that night. That Mac had been the McCoy Percy had been referring to.

Her father annotated the turns to take and circled the spot where they'd find the camp.

Rocco studied the map. "How big is the camp?"

"Nowhere near our size. He's got a much smaller outfit. About ten cabins up there. Some of his people prefer to rough it in tents when the weather permits."

"How many people?" Rocco asked.

"I don't know. I'd estimate thirty to forty."

"You buy your weapons from him?"

"I do. He has an overseas connection. Other than that, I don't know how his end of the business works. After we make a transaction, one of his guys meets Alex at a predesignated spot that routinely changes for safety purposes."

"You don't mind losing your source of weapons?" Rocco was still skeptical.

"As you've seen for yourself, we're well stocked."
Indeed, they were.

"Any suggestions on how I should handle this with my uncle?" Mercy asked.

"Just be yourself." Marshall smiled at her. "And stick to the story. The two of you are to be married. Rocco's radical views and inclination for violence made him a bad fit for my commune and I thought that Cormac's would be better."

Alex returned, carrying a tray of food. "The kitchen already had three-bean chili prepared for lunch. It's been cooking all morning," he said, setting down the tray on the desk. He handed Mercy a bowl, napkin and spoon.

She took a seat facing the desk.

Rocco chose his own bowl when Alex offered him one and sat beside Mercy.

Marshall directed the man to pull up an extra chair from the corner and to sit next to him. They said grace while Rocco listened and then dug in.

"This is outstanding," Marshall said after his third spoonful, and Rocco reluctantly agreed, not missing the meat in the dish. "Such depth of flavor. I must compliment the kitchen staff during our lunch hour. I don't do it often enough. Everyone works so hard." The rambling continued, filling in the awkward silence as Alex's gaze bounced between Rocco and Mercy. "See, we can all be mature adults and act with civility."

Coughing, Mercy put her bowl on the desk. Her face was flushed. She put a hand to her throat. Scratched her cheek with the other. The coughing turned to a wheeze.

"Mercy?" Marshall leaned forward, peering at her.

Rocco clasped her shoulder. "Are you okay?"

She shook her head and stood. "Something's wrong. Can't breathe," she uttered through a rasp.

Red bumps and welts began appearing on her face and arms, probably beneath her clothes as well.

"Oh, God." Marshall's bowl fell from his hands, clattering to the floor. He jumped to his feet. "She's having an allergic reaction."

With her hands clutching her throat, Mercy staggered backward.

"No, no, no. She's having an anaphylactic reaction." Marshall ran to her.

Rocco lurched to his feet in terrified shock.

Frozen, he could hardly believe what was happening, Mercy struggling for air, her body succumbing to the allergen in a deadly spiral of symptoms. His heart lodged in his throat, his hands growing clammy, his muscles tightening with fear. For her. He had to do something to help her.

"She's only allergic to peanuts," Marshall said, "but I don't allow them on the compound. I don't understand." His gaze flew to the bowl of chili and then to Alex.

The young man sat silent and still, staring at Mercy.

"What did you do!" Marshall howled.

Mercy gasped for breath, her wheezes shortening. Her face started to swell. She swayed and collapsed, but Rocco lunged, catching her.

Horror punched through him like a hot blade in his gut.

Marshall dropped to his knees, taking her from him into his lap. Rocco held her hand. Her slender fingers tightened around him.

"Calm down, sweetheart," Marshall said. "Don't panic. Try to breathe."

"Where's her EpiPen? Does she carry one?" Rocco asked.

"It's in her room. At the top of the stairs. Third room on the right. She keeps it in the top drawer of her dresser."

Rocco leaped up. He raced down the hall. Flew up the stairs. Stormed into her bedroom. He yanked open the drawer and rifled through her underwear. Tossing the cotton items to the floor, he searched for the yellow and black injector. He emptied the drawer.

But it wasn't there.

In less than a minute, he scoured through the other drawers, turning her room upside down. Still, no EpiPen.

A hard knot of dread congealed in the pit of his stomach. He bolted back down the stairs and tore into the office. Marshall had Mercy cradled in his lap.

"It's not there," Rocco said, his heart hammering painfully at his rib cage. "I couldn't find it."

Her father's eyes flared wide with alarm. On his knees, he whirled toward Alex. "Where is it? What did you do with it?"

Tears leaked from the corners of Mercy's eyes. Her lips were starting to turn blue.

It was happening so very, very fast. Right in front of his eyes the woman he loved was dying.

Rocco charged over to Alex and snatched him up from the chair by his shirt. "Tell me what you did with it."

Alex's gaze stayed laser-focused on Mercy.

"Are you insane?" Marshall screamed. "She's going to be your wife."

"No, she isn't." Alex shook his head slowly, his eyes glazed, like he was in a trance. "She's going to sleep with him and never come back."

How could Alex be so low, so malicious? Only a small, weak man would do such a thing.

"She's already slept with him, you idiot." Marshall rocked back and forth with his daughter in his arms. "And she came back anyway. What does it matter if she has one or two nights with this nonbeliever, but spends the rest of her life with you. I told you to have faith, you fool!"

"If she dies, you die. Painfully. Slowly," Rocco swore, ready to follow through, but the threat didn't faze Alex. Fury and fear hit Rocco so intensely that for a second everything blurred. "Where is the damn Epi?"

"She will return from the mountains," Marshall said, clinging to Mercy. "I've foreseen it. But you must let her live." He tipped his head back and muttered something that sounded like a prayer. "There are more EpiPens in the basement. Rocco, they're in the bunker."

"I moved them." Alex's voice was low, his gaze unwavering from Mercy. "You won't find it in time."

Rocco cocked his fist back, prepared to break the man's nose. He was willing to go so far as every bone in his body. "Tell us where you put it, or I'll beat it out of you."

Alex didn't cringe, didn't even flick a glance at him. His fists were tight at his sides, his expression unyielding, his eyes dark and full of a deadly determination.

Impotent rage surged through Rocco. He could hurt this man, beat him into a bloody pulp and it wouldn't do any good.

Because this rash, bitter coward seemed unconcerned with dying himself—so long as Mercy died first.

There had to be something they could do. Rocco wasn't going to stand by and let this happen. He could run to the infirmary and see if they had any epinephrine, but as fast as Mercy's reaction was happening, he wouldn't make it there and back in time.

Think, think.

The foundation of a cult was power and control. If anyone still had an iota of influence over Alex, it was Empyrean.

Rocco turned to Mercy's father. "Make him see reason." He looked back to Alex. "What is it you want?" Rocco pressed him.

Alex nodded at Mercy. "Her. For starters."

"You *will* let her live," Marshall said, his voice ringing with authority. "Give me the EpiPen. You have it, don't you? Give it to me!" he cried. "If you don't, so help me, you will walk in darkness, forever banished, your soul lost."

Alex took a step forward, but Rocco's tight grip stopped him. "Want me to save her or not?" He knocked Rocco's hand away, knelt at Mercy's side, and leaned over her. "Do you remember what I told you in the car?" he asked her. "Blink once for yes if you do."

Gasping for air, fighting to breathe, Mercy gave one long blink, and more tears streamed down her face.

"You better come back to me," Alex said.

Mercy's eyes fluttered closed. Her hands slipped from her throat, and she went limp.

"Hurry up!" Rocco yelled.

Alex tugged up his pant leg and pulled the injector from his sock.

Marshall snatched the shot of epinephrine from his hand, yanked off the blue cap and pressed the orange tip to her thigh. He threw the used injector to the floor and rocked his daughter in his arms.

Coming up alongside her, Rocco gave Alex a fierce look that had him scuttling up and out of the way. Rocco took her hand in his. "How long does it take to work?"

"Any minute. Any minute now." Marshall looked down at his daughter, his face fraught with panic. "Come on, Mercy. Breathe. *Please*, open your eyes."

Rocco bit out a curse under his breath. He couldn't lose her. Because of some vindictive weasel. They hadn't even been given a chance.

Mercy sucked in a wheezing breath, opening her eyes. The color returned to her lips and cheeks. She squeezed his hand, her gaze finding his.

Relief pummeled him in a wave. She was going to be okay. She was going to live.

Marshall hugged her tight against his chest. He kissed her forehead and slid Mercy into Rocco's arms. Her father got up and hurried to his desk. He picked up the phone. "I need security immediately."

"Empyrean," Alex said. "I was desperate."

"I know." Marshall nodded. "You weren't yourself. You acted rashly and almost killed her."

"But I didn't," Alex said. "Her life was in my hands, and I chose not to take it."

Guards ran into the room, led by Shawn.

"Secure Alex in an unburdening room," Marshall said, "and help Mercy to one of the vehicles."

Holding her in his arms, Rocco stood. "I'll carry her."

Marshall nodded. "One of you, run to the infirmary. Tell the doctor Mercy went into anaphylactic shock. We need him to set up an IV for her in an SUV. She'll need fluids and vitamins to help her recover and an extra EpiPen for her journey just in case."

Shawn tapped one man on the shoulder, issuing orders. The guy ran from the room. Shawn and the other guard each took one of Alex's arms.

"Get him out of my sight." Marshall waved them off with a dismissive hand.

They hauled Alex out of the office. Rocco glared at him. He'd make him pay later, but he suspected Marshall would do the job first.

Marshall grabbed the map from the desk and turned to Rocco. "I'll walk you down to a vehicle." He put a hand to Rocco's back as they left the house. "Sometimes when the medicine wears off, it's possible for the symptoms to return. You'll have an extra shot of epinephrine if they do. Watch her closely. When you get to the camp, stick to the story. Mac has always had a soft spot for Mercy. Play on that and you'll both be fine."

"If this is a setup," Rocco said, "Mercy will be hurt by it." He was now even more reluctant to involve her in her weakened state. Everything about this operation felt wrong. But there were so many lives at stake.

"I almost lost my daughter minutes ago. Trust me. I have no intention of endangering her."

As much as Marshall might have believed his own words, Rocco put no stock in them. Her father couldn't be trusted.

Chapter Fourteen

Marshall waited until after the commune had eaten lunch and his temper had subsided before going to the unburdening room.

Alex had been unhinged. There was no telling what he might do next.

Marshall nodded for Shawn to unlock the door. He stepped inside. "You may leave us," he said, and Shawn closed the door behind him. Clasping his hands, he stared at Alex.

His *son* sat handcuffed to the bed, calm and composed. Gone was the remorse in him, replaced by a steely glint in his eyes.

"The punishment for an act of violence committed against an anointed member of the commune is banishment," Marshall said.

Alex stood, the chain of his cuffs clinking against the bed rail, his head held high. "That's true. But Mercy isn't anointed. Is she?"

It was an undisputable fact. Still… "She is my daughter."

"And I am your son! You chose me. Over any other that could've been yours. You took me under your wing.

Brought me into your house. Molded me in your image. It's me you're grooming to succeed you. Not *her*. She may wear white, and you may have us call her a leader, but it's one big joke. She's never proven her faith or devotion by taking her vows. Because deep down we both know she's a nonbeliever."

Marshall prowled up to him and slapped his face. "How dare you?"

Licking the blood from his split lip, Alex smiled. "How dare I speak the truth? You've given her allowances that no one else is permitted. When it comes to her there is a blatant double standard. Everyone loves Mercy—she radiates light—but they all see the truth and whisper about your hypocrisy."

"You tried to kill her!" He took a calming breath, regaining his composure. "Why would you do such a thing?"

"Because I remember," Alex said, not making any sense.

"Remember what?"

"You know." A long, slow grin spread over Alex's face. "The reason Ayanna left but Mercy stayed."

A sudden chill swept over Marshall as though someone had walked over his grave. He turned away and stared at the symbol of the Shining Light painted on the wall. Alex couldn't possibly know. Even if he did, Marshall would not speak of it. Refused to think about it.

"If I wanted to kill her," Alex said, "she would be dead. I tested her."

"You what?" Pivoting on his heel to face him, Marshall shook his head at the ravings of this madman, trying to spin his way out of this. "Others who have done far less have been banished."

"Before you can banish me, this must be brought before the council of elders. I'll argue that I haven't violated any bylaws. I will confess to putting crushed peanuts into the nonbeliever's chili. To test her faith," he said, his dark eyes glittering with unfathomable devilry. "After learning that Mercy—the woman who agreed to a courtship with me in front of everyone—ran off with an undercover ATF agent sent to spy on us and slept with him. In the end, I chose to save her, despite her transgressions. Doubt plagues your daughter like a disease. While I, your chosen son, took my vows to the commune at sixteen." He pointed to the tattoo at the base of his throat. "When will Mercy *McCoy* take hers?"

Marshall stared at Alex, bowled over that he was responsible for creating this monster.

This was a delicate situation. The issue of his daughter not taking her vows to the Shining Light had reached a tipping point. Sooner than he had hoped.

Commitment was their power. Mercy was a weak link. A liability. This problem and Marshall's hypocrisy would become the center of the discussion among the elders and the commune.

An act of violence against someone who was not anointed wasn't a punishable offence. He had designed the bylaws that way so his people need not ever fear defending themselves against someone from the outside world. For nearly three decades, he had kept peace on the compound.

As much as he hated to admit it, taking Alex in front

of the council on this matter would be tricky. Everything would be questioned. Marshall's authority. His judgment. His contradictory and preferential treatment of his daughter. As well as her conduct with that agent of chaos.

The only way Marshall could ever truly protect Mercy was for her to take her vows and be anointed. He had thought his excuses for her would expire on her twenty-fifth birthday. Instead, tomorrow she'd have to choose. Become a Starlight or one of the fallen.

But he still had to deal with Alex.

My son. My monster. "You must be punished."

"I will not go quietly into the dark. I'll fight tooth and nail to stay. I'll make sure things get messy. You will not walk away spotless. I promise you that!" Alex roared, jerking at his handcuffs, the chain rattling. "Let me stay. Protect me as I've protected you…and all your secrets."

There were other things he could do to Alex that didn't require the purview of the council. "Flagellation will be your punishment. I'll do it myself."

Alex smiled. Even though flesh would be torn from his back with a whip, he smiled as though he'd been given a gift. "After I've atoned, I want to hear how you're so certain that Mercy will be back."

Oh, ye of little faith.

His daughter would return before the eclipse. Marshall was more than the prophet.

He was a man who always had a plan.

Chapter Fifteen

A warm hand rubbed Mercy's leg, rousing her.

"I think we're almost there," Rocco said.

Yawning, she looked around at the pines and snow-capped peaks. With the higher elevation the temperature would be much cooler.

It was a good thing Rocco had swung by the motel and picked up their things after he had given his boss the details of where they were headed. Charlie had packed a couple of sweaters for her, and she'd need them.

Mercy pulled out the needle for the IV from her hand.

"How are you feeling?"

"The concoction in the IV bag and the sleep made a world of difference. I'm much better now."

"You look better. No more swelling. No welts or red marks." A small smile tugged at his mouth. "Gave me quite a scare."

Alex had terrified them all. He'd watched her with a cool detachment as her airway squeezed tight, closing off all her oxygen. Her skin had turned clammy and itchy. She'd struggled for every strangled breath, her lungs burning, a scream building that she hadn't been able to release. It felt like an anvil had been on her chest. Darkness had closed in around the edges of her vision.

Rocco had been frantic, doing what he could to save her. While Alex had loomed over her, reminding her of who he was and what he was capable of.

I'd rather see you dead than living in darkness with that man.

His vicious words rang in her head, flooding her veins with ice. She might have underestimated his capacity for cruelty, but not anymore.

"I can't go back to the compound." She didn't want to flee like a traitor. To be designated as "fallen." To never again associate with the people who she called family. To not say a proper goodbye. But she didn't see any other way. "Unless I take my vows, there's no place for me in the commune." She'd put it off for as long as she could, wrestling with the hardest decision of her life. "But I can't do it."

And it was only a matter of time before Alex tried to kill her again because she would never be his. She couldn't give him that opportunity by returning to the compound.

"For what it's worth, I think you're making the right choice." He clutched her hand. "It was good of Charlie to say those things to you last night. I just want to make it clear that neither of us wants you to think that you have to depend on me to make this transition. Of course, I'm here for you. We'll both help you in any way that makes you comfortable. We have a lot of friends in town who'll support you."

"That means a lot." More than he realized. The idea of leaving the commune had seemed too big, too final.

Too far out of reach. With assistance from Charlie, Brian and most especially Rocco—regardless of how deep his feelings truly ran, there was no doubt he cared about her—she could envision a different life.

One she desperately wanted.

"No pressure or anything," he said, "but I hope you won't walk away from this. From us. The possibility of what we could be together. It's real for me. I never lied about my feelings for you. After almost losing you earlier, I'll do whatever it takes to prove to you that I'm in this for the long haul. If you want me."

She didn't answer. Didn't dare. He was offering everything she wanted. But deep down she couldn't shake the niggling fear that he was smoothing things over with her only to help sell their cover story once they got to the camp.

A man dressed in camo stepped out of the tree line into the middle of the road. He held a rifle aimed at their windshield.

Movement off to the left drew their gazes.

A second man with a full beard, also wearing head-to-toe camo, approached the driver's-side door with a rifle slung over his shoulder. "You two lost?"

Rocco rolled down the window. "We're here to see Cormac McCoy."

"I don't know who that is."

Mercy leaned over, giving him a full view of her face. "I'm Mercy. Marshall McCoy's daughter. Can you tell my uncle I'm here?"

Eyeing them, the guy stepped back and pulled out a handheld radio. A squawk resounded as he keyed it, but he was too far away for them to hear what he said.

"Tight security," Rocco said. "At least we know the directions are solid."

The man came back to the car. He held out the radio and keyed it. "Go ahead, sir, they can hear you."

"If you're really my niece," a deep male voice said over the other end, "what did you used to call me when you were little?"

Panic fogged her brain, her thoughts stumbling together. "It was nineteen years ago. You can't expect me to remember that?"

"But I do. My little nugget wouldn't forget. Whoever you are, get gone before you get shot."

Nugget stirred up a memory. Taking her back to a time when she'd only eat chickpea nuggets and macaroni and cheese. In her head, she heard her voice, like a child, calling him something that sounded silly. "Wait, please," she said. "Uncle Mac and cheese." That wasn't right. "No, no. Uncle Macaroni."

"Let them through," Cormac said.

The guy holding the radio whistled to the other one and he moved out of the road, letting them pass.

Rocco drove down the single lane dirt path about a mile until the camp came into sight. Another armed man opened a tall wooden gate that was made from logs the size of telephone poles and waved them in.

There were seven trucks parked on one side near the entrance and some horses corralled on the other side.

Men carrying weapons, ammo and cases of something she couldn't identify were loading them in the backs of four of the larger vehicles. They were definitely in the middle of preparing for something big.

Trepidation trickled through her at the attention their presence garnered. Wary glances and narrowed eyes.

"This is the place," Rocco said, "where my informant must've been."

"How do you know?"

"The men who killed my CI and ran him off the road were driving that truck." He gestured with a subtle hike of his chin to a heavy-duty black one that had dual rear wheels.

Two stickers were plastered on the rear bumper.

Both depicted images she recognized. "Those symbols are from our teachings."

"What do they mean?"

"The iridescent silver tree represents enlightenment, but through toil and struggle. The bolt of lightning slicing through the red block signifies *vis major*. An overwhelming force that causes damage or disruption. Like an act of God."

He parked the car. "Are you ready for this?"

"Let's get it over with and get out of here." She reached into the back seat, grabbing her duffel and pulled out a sweater. Putting it on, she looked around.

The camp was in a valley encircled by peaks and trees. The surrounding mountains probably did a good job of protecting them from the icy wind in the winter.

There were small log cabins and tents set up throughout the level grassy area. The front door of the cabin at the center of the camp opened. A man with long blond hair and regal features similar to her father's, but with enough facial hair for a grizzly, made his way in their direction.

"Hey." Rocco cupped her chin, turning her face toward him.

He brought his mouth to hers. She closed her eyes for a brief moment, enjoying the electric sensation that sizzled through her body the moment their lips touched. He really kissed her. Not a quick, appropriate peck merely for show. This was hot and wet, full of such passion and desire. All of which she wanted from him. He plunged deeper, and she sank into the kiss that was oh-so-sweet.

And over far too soon when he pulled away.

"Rocco."

He brushed his thumb across her bottom lip. "The best lies are rooted in truth. Remember that."

A knock at the window had her spinning in her seat. She looked at her uncle and gave a shaky smile.

Opening her door, Cormac noticed the empty IV bag hanging from the grab handle above her head.

She climbed out. Cool air sliced through her, making her shiver. "Hi, Uncle Mac." Stepping forward, she shoved the door closed behind her.

"Well, aren't you all grown-up," he said, his face lighting up. He ran a tentative hand over her hair, taking her in as if dazed, like she wasn't real. "Come here, nugget." He opened his arms.

Mercy walked into the embrace, and he wrapped her in a bear hug, lifting her feet from the ground. She remembered this. His fondness. His hugs, warm and tight and nothing like her father's.

Setting her down, he looked her over again. Then his gaze shifted. "And who is this big fella?"

"Rocco Sharp." He proffered his hand. "Pleased to meet you."

They shook.

"He's my intended," she said, the words heating her face.

"Is that so?" Cormac gave a slow, steady nod. "What brings you two all the way up here?"

"Can we speak inside?" She zipped up the sweater. "Get something warm to drink. Maybe a bite to eat." Her appetite had returned with gusto. She had a fast metabolism and shouldn't go too long without food.

"Right this way." Her uncle roped an arm around her shoulder and led them to the cabin he'd come out of.

Inside, the furnishings were simple—most appeared handmade—and it was warm from the fire in the hearth. A savory smell permeated the area from a pot on the stove. The kitchen opened onto a small dining area and a modest living room.

"Hey, baby," her uncle called.

A door opened. A woman with black hair streaked with silver fashioned into two long braids strode into the room.

"This is my niece Mercy and her fiancé, Rocco," Mac said. "And this is my wife, Sue Ellen."

"Welcome," Sue Ellen said curtly without a smile. She was a thin woman, maybe a little older than Mac, with watery green eyes and a weathered face. "Can I get you something to drink or eat?"

"Yes, please." Mercy set her bag on the floor. "Both if it's not too much trouble."

"Will cheese sandwiches and lentil stew do for you?" Sue Ellen asked.

Mercy nodded. "That's perfect."

"Thank you, ma'am," Rocco said.

"Either of you have a cell phone on you?" Mac asked.

Rocco pulled out the phone he'd purchased at the service station.

Her uncle grabbed a gray pouch from a hook on the wall and opened it. Inside was shiny, metallic material. "Drop it in," he said, and Rocco did.

"What is that?" Mercy asked.

"Faraday pouch. Blocks all signals. RFID, FM radio, GPS, cellular, Bluetooth, 5G, Wi-Fi, you name it." He sealed it and hung it back on the hook. "Get comfortable." Mac waved them over to chairs at the dining table, and they sat. "I'll get you some hot cider," he said, picking up a clay jug and moving to the stove.

Sue Ellen took cheese from the fridge. She sliced it along with the bread and made sandwiches. Grabbing a wooden ladle, she poured soup from the pot on the stove into bowls.

Beside her was a shelf lined with labeled mason jars filled with various herbs and plants. Sassafras. Ginger. Lavender. Catnip. Willow bark. Chamomile. All could be used for different ailments. Mercy wondered if they relied on herbal medicine.

It would make sense with them being so far from a pharmacy and hospital, but she expected that they also had supplies for a serious emergency.

Sue Ellen placed food on the table.

"Tell us, what brings you here?" Cormac asked, setting down four mugs of warm cider.

Hesitating, Mercy wasn't sure how to start. She wasn't the best liar. This was their opportunity to sell their story, and she didn't want to blow it.

"Empyrean didn't think I was the right fit for the

Shining Light," Rocco said, as easily as though it was the truth, and in a way it was. "He thought I might be better suited for the Brotherhood."

"Not right for his commune, but he sanctioned this union with his daughter?" Cormac asked, suspicion heavy in his tone as well as his expression.

Mercy looked at Rocco. She pressed her palm to his cheek and ran her fingers through his hair, a smile she couldn't help spreading on her face. "My father didn't make the match, but he didn't stop it." Sliding closer to him, she glanced at her uncle. "He saw how we were drawn to each other. How kind and devoted he is to me," she said, and Rocco slid an arm around her shoulder, tucking her close to his side. "As far as I'm concerned, he's the only one for me." The line between truth and lies became even murkier.

Wiping her hands on an apron, Sue Ellen sat next to Mac, listening, watching, assessing.

"Were you banished?" her uncle asked.

"No, sir," Rocco said. "Things sort of came to a head on the compound."

Mac raised an eyebrow. "In what way?"

"The FBI planted an informant in the commune," Rocco said. "When he was discovered, I thought we should've killed him. And I didn't want to stop there. Who do they think they are? Infiltrating us, spying on us, trying to take away our civil liberties."

Mercy eyed him, mesmerized at what he was saying, at how he started taking on a whole new persona.

Cormac slapped a hand down on the table. "You are one hundred percent correct," he said, pointing a finger at him. "It's high time we took our country back.

You know those Feds are conspiring to strip us of our rights, starting with the unalienable one to keep and bear arms. Once we're rendered defenseless, they plan to absorb Americans into their tyrannical new world order government."

Rocco and Sue Ellen both nodded.

Lowering her head, Mercy nibbled on her food. She figured if she kept her mouth full, then the less she'd have to say.

"The no-good ATF seized a shipment of my weapons in Colorado." Mac took a sip of his cider. "Now they're stealing money from my pocket and taking food from the mouths of my people. We're going to teach them a lesson they won't ever forget. The streets will run red with blood tomorrow."

An icy chill jolted through her veins. She didn't recall her uncle being violent or paranoid. Clearly, he was both.

Sue Ellen gripped Mac's forearm, and he stopped talking. "Which makes me wonder about the timing of your arrival. Why didn't you come last month?" his wife asked. "Why not in two days? What brings you to us specifically *today*?"

"Empyrean took the full moon and the eclipse as a sign that it was the right time," Rocco said.

Mercy tensed. That explanation would only raise more questions than it would answer. Her father would've used the full moon and the shedding ceremony to make the announcement, choosing to send them the day after. Not before.

As she suspected, Sue Ellen's eyes hardened like

ice and Cormac crossed his arms as he leaned back in his chair.

Mercy set her sandwich down and slipped her hand onto Rocco's leg under the table. "Honey, I think we have to be honest about what made us expedite our plans and come today." She turned to Sue Ellen and then Cormac. "Uncle Mac, do you remember Alex?"

Scratching his beard, he nodded. "Yeah. Of course. The weird little boy who used to follow you around like a lost puppy."

Puppies were cute and cuddly. She'd always thought of Alex more as a shadow. Dark, silent, and only there when the light was blocked.

"He tried to kill me today."

"What?" Alarm tightened across his and Sue Ellen's faces.

"It's true," Rocco said. "He poisoned her. Put peanuts in her food. She went into anaphylactic shock." His grip on her shoulder tightened. "I was terrified I was going to lose her. Almost did, too. I've never felt so helpless in my entire life, watching her slip away. It was horrific."

"That's why there's an IV bag in your car?" Cormac asked.

"Yes. To help me recover. My father wanted us to get out of there as soon as possible. Alex is insane."

"He's obsessed with her," Rocco added. "He can't handle seeing her with someone else."

Her uncle leaned forward, resting his forearms on the table. "Then it's good that you came here."

His wife nodded. "Coveting anything or anyone above the Light is to make it your master. It was best to get out of that man's sight. If he wants you that badly, he would've been bound to try again."

"You're welcome to stay. We've got a spare bedroom." Cormac hiked a thumb over his shoulder at one of the doors. "Are you both okay with the one bed? It's only full-size. If not, I can have a tent and cot set up for you, Rocco."

"No, that won't be necessary," Mercy said, rubbing Rocco's thigh. "We'd prefer to sleep together. Isn't that right?"

Smiling as though he'd suddenly become bashful, Rocco lowered his head but met her eyes. "I can't keep my hands off you, so it's whatever you want, sweetheart," he said, the deep timbre of his voice sliding through her. He stroked a lock of hair back from her cheek, trailing the pads of his fingers across her skin.

Her breath caught. She tried and failed to ignore a pang of longing. So she decided to stop trying and kissed him. Soft and quick.

Rocco cleared his throat. "Provided your uncle allows us to share a bed under his roof."

Staring into his warm brown eyes was almost hypnotic. She was certainly under his spell. Even though he'd used her, lied to her and might still be manipulating her for the sake of his mission, she couldn't wait to make love with him again.

"Your father aware that you two have had relations?" her uncle asked. "I recall him being quite protective of you."

"He is," she said, a little annoyed at how her father and uncle treated her as though she was a child. "I've never hidden anything from him."

"Well, you're to be married. What happens behind closed doors, stays there." Her uncle Mac smirked. "There's only one bathroom in here. Compost toilet. All our power is solar, and we get our water from a catchment system. Not the fancy digs you're used to at the compound, but the room is yours for as long as you want it, or until we can get you two your own cabin."

"Much appreciated. We'll earn our keep," Rocco said. "I'd love to start by helping you with whatever you've got planned tomorrow. Giving those Feds payback sounds good to me."

"Happy to have an extra gunman," her uncle said. "Especially if you're a good shot."

"That I am. What exactly is the target?" Rocco asked.

Sue Ellen whispered in Cormac's ear.

"We'll get into specifics tomorrow," Mac said. "You'll have to excuse our caution. We had an informant weasel his way into our camp a few days ago. We're still a bit on edge."

"Oh, yeah, how did you deal with it?" Rocco asked.

"Same way you wanted to handle your spy." A sinister laugh rolled from Cormac. "Barry and Dennis took care of that traitor."

"Good for you." Rocco held up his mug, his body language mirroring that of her uncle's. "You sent those Feds a clear message they were messing with the wrong people."

The two of them toasted. Mercy thought she might be sick, but she kept eating.

"For now," Mac said, "I'll introduce you around and show you the camp."

They finished their food and headed outside.

"I didn't want to say anything in front of Sue Ellen." Cormac looked back at the cabin, keeping his voice low. "But I can see why Alex lost his mind over you. You're the spitting image of your mother." He gave a low whistle. "She was the prettiest woman I ever did see."

Her heart skipped a beat. "She left the compound the same day you did, right?"

"An unfortunate coincidence."

"Do you know what happened to her? Where she went?"

His brow furrowed with confusion. "You don't know?"

"Know what?"

"I gave her some money to help her get started. She eventually moved to Wayward Bluffs, but I heard she went back to Laramie every week. Hoping to see you. Run into you. Convince you to leave the Shining Light. Sometime around your twentieth birthday she assumed you had taken your vows and gave up hope."

Her father hadn't allowed her to start going into town to help recruit people until she had turned twenty-one. What if that had been by design?

What if she had missed her chance? What if she never saw her again? "Do you have her address or a phone number?"

"No. But that's how she wanted it. With as much distance from your father and the Brotherhood as possible."

A sinking feeling took hold of her. It must've shown on her face because Rocco brought her into a tight embrace.

"It's going to be okay," he whispered in her ear.

She breathed through her disappointment, hoping that was true.

With a protective arm still around her, they continued to walk.

"Now that I think of it," her uncle said, "I believe she worked as a waitress for a while. A restaurant on Third Street. Delgado's, if I'm not mistaken. It was a long time ago, but they might have a phone number or forwarding address on file."

Delgado's. She'd passed the restaurant every time she went to the USD, venturing into the same orbit her mother had once occupied. The knowledge made her chest ache.

"Why would my mom leave me like that? I was so young. I needed her." She still did.

"Your dad didn't give her any choice. She wanted out. He agreed on the condition that you stayed behind. With him. It was complicated, and not an easy decision for her. But she felt like she couldn't breathe anymore. Like your father and the movement were suffocating her." He stroked her hair. "I'm glad you're here. She'd want me to help you."

She understood that claustrophobic feeling. The sensation of the walls closing in, her world shrinking, getting smaller and smaller, while the one thing at the center of her life only got bigger, greater. Stronger. That one person.

Empyrean.

Mac scratched his beard. "Your allergic reaction, going into anaphylactic shock like that, is odd since peanuts aren't allowed on the compound anymore. Déjà vu. Alex must've had them stashed for a while."

"Déjà vu?" Rocco stopped walking. "How so?"

"Well, Ayanna was allergic, too. She went into ana-phylactic shock once. I didn't see it, but I heard about it."

"When did that happen?" she asked.

Mac shrugged. "Maybe two or three months before we left. It shook her up pretty fierce. She got really quiet after that. Stopped talking about leaving and taking you with her. I would've sworn that she had decided to stay. Then the day me and my guys were rolling out, she said a hurried goodbye to you and caught a ride out the gates with us. Didn't take one thing with her but the clothes on her back. Left everything else behind."

Including me.

"Is it possible that Marshall did that to her on pur-pose?" Rocco asked.

"What do you mean?" Mac grew still, staring at him in horror. "Put peanuts in her food?"

"Yeah. To scare her into staying," Rocco said, his voice just audible enough to be heard over the rush of blood pounding in Mercy's head.

"No way. He loved her." Mac shook his head force-fully in either conviction or denial. "If anything, he became more protective of her and you." He tipped his head toward her. "That's when he banned peanuts from the compound and had all those black walnut trees planted. Your dad even took you to Denver, to a fancy facility, to have you tested for allergies."

She vaguely remembered the trip. He'd called it an adventure. She'd cried when the doctor had pricked her with needles and begged for her mother, but she wasn't there. Only her father, Alex, who held her hand, and a woman whose name she couldn't remember.

It was a lot to take in. Much more than she wanted

to process right now while there were bigger things going on. Lives were at stake, including theirs, if she and Rocco didn't pull this off.

Everything was a blur as her uncle showed them around the camp, making endless introductions as they shook hands or waved hello and answered questions. Thankfully, Cormac and Rocco did most of the talking.

All she could think about was her mother. What she looked like. The smell of her hair. The sound of her voice. How difficult it must've been for her, forced to decide between raising her child or having her freedom. An impossible choice.

Did her father tip the scales, threaten and poison her, coerce her into leaving without her child?

The idea was too monstrous to be the truth. But Alex had claimed to love Mercy, too, and look at what he had done.

The light shifted, sliding from twilight to dim, snapping her out of her thoughts.

Holding a lantern, her uncle led them into a cave. "Here is our weapons cache," he said. There were stacks upon stacks of crates with a lightning bolt singed onto the side and metal trunks. "You want it, we've got it. Rifles. Anything from an AR-15 to AK-47. Shotguns—double-barreled break-action to sawed off. Submachine guns to .50 caliber. Ghost pistols. Hollow point bullets to armor-piercing. Rocket-propelled grenades. High and low explosives as well as blasting agents."

A jagged bolt of fear ripped through Mercy, drawing every muscle tight. She stared at the cache of weapons, her eyes bulging in shock.

On the compound, they had a whole lot of guns, for defense only, but this…

This was the next-level. This was how wars were fought and won in small countries. This meant the death of countless innocent people. She'd never seen anything like this arsenal.

"Wow, this is seriously impressive," Rocco said, his voice filled with awe. "I can't wait to see what you have in store for tomorrow."

Cormac smiled. In the amber light from the lantern casting shadows on his face, he looked like the devil. "We're going to rain down hell on them."

A pervasive sense of dread coiled through her, and she couldn't imagine how this was all going to end.

Chapter Sixteen

Lying in bed, Rocco's thoughts churned. Cormac McCoy had a bunch of hardened survivalists riled up and ready to shed blood tomorrow. It was a wonder how the Brotherhood of Silver Light had gone under the radar for so long.

Thanks to Mercy's gutsy move, risking her life asking for her father's help, the Brotherhood could no longer hide.

But Rocco still didn't know what their intended target was or how he'd notify Nash once he did. The only thing certain was that if he failed, a lot of people were going to die.

Percy had been right. Something big and awful was in the works. Rocco wouldn't let his death be in vain. He had to stop whatever was planned and keep Mercy safe, one way or another.

In the next room, he heard the faucet shut off. A door creaked open.

"Thank you again," Mercy said.

Sue Ellen and Cormac responded from the living room, where Rocco had last seen them sitting in front of the fire.

"Good night." Ducking into their room, Mercy closed the door, and a different tension invaded his body.

She padded over to the bed, set her toiletries on the nightstand beside the burning candle and undressed. For a moment, she just stood there, watching him taking in the sight of her. He was mesmerized by her beauty and grace. Her shimmering hair captured the light, making it sparkle. He was intensely aware of everything about her, her creamy skin, soft curves, the flush creeping over her face, down to her feminine scent.

The ache inside him for the woman he would protect with his last breath flared anew. He wanted her. Under him. On top of him. Building a life with him.

Mercy peeled back the covers and slipped into the bed. "Why are you wearing so many clothes?"

She tugged at his T-shirt. He sat up, letting her pull it over his head.

"Because I didn't know if you were serious about us doing more than sleeping," he whispered. "I couldn't tell if it was part of the act."

"It wasn't." She pressed her palm to his stomach and ran her hand up his torso.

Her touch struck him like a flame to kindling. Hunger poured through him.

"Were you pretending," she said, straddling his hips and drawing her face close to his, "when you said you couldn't keep your hands off me?"

"No."

She brushed her lips across his in a slow, seductive caress. "Then why aren't you touching me?"

Good question.

He locked an arm around her waist, bringing her

flush against him. Their heated bodies pressed together, skin to skin. His other hand he buried in the silky softness of her hair as he captured her mouth. All his thoughts about tomorrow dissipated in the kiss.

Rocking her hips, rubbing her core on the ridge of his erection, she made a low, desperate sound that ignited his own need instantly, sending a tremor through his muscles. He sucked tenderly at her lower lip before stroking his tongue across it and delving back into her mouth.

She grabbed his wrist, pulling his hand from her hip, and shoved it exactly where she wanted him. Down between her legs, cupping her. He found slick, wet warmth.

They groaned at the same time, the intense heat between them building higher. She twined her fingers in his hair, a shudder rolling through her, thighs trembling as she rubbed against his fingers.

He was lost in the sensation of her. All liquid fire in his arms. Primal need. Taking what she wanted. And he intended to give her everything, showing her without words how much he desired her. Cared for her. He wanted to make love to her until she was breathless and ready to come out of her skin. Make her burn the way he did for her.

"The cabin is small, and the walls are thin," he said low. "Sound will carry."

"We've got to sell our story. Engaged and hot for each other. Let's give them something worth hearing."

Happy to oblige, he flipped their bodies, putting her beneath him, and kissed her chin. Licked her throat while his hands moved over hot skin that was smooth as silk. He took his time with every warm, slow caress, refusing to be rushed. Delighting in the soft whimpering sounds she made. Enjoying her breasts one after the other until she was pleading and squirming, parting her thighs wide for him. He moved southward, kissing his way down between her legs. Glancing up at her, the molten heat in her eyes made him smile. Then he dipped his head—her fingers curling in his hair, her hand guiding his mouth to that sweet spot—and he settled his tongue on the sensitive bundle of nerves that drove her wild. She screamed his name, splintering to pieces, her cry like the crack of a whip to the desire lashing him.

He was ready to burst, but he held tight to his control since he was just getting started.

THE NEXT DAY, an unseasonably warm spell had hiked the temperature ten degrees higher. Mercy didn't need a sweater, but she wore one anyway, as part of the plan.

Rocco needed her to get his phone from the Faraday pouch without Sue Ellen noticing. Mercy looked out the window of the kitchen.

The men were huddled up outside around a table busy making Molotov cocktails.

Apparently, the RPGs were worth too much to waste in an attack on the Feds. Gasoline, bottles, fuses and bullets were cheap.

She finished washing and drying the breakfast dishes. Taking off the apron, she turned around and looked at Sue Ellen, who was wrapping up food for the men to take with them.

"I have a headache," Mercy said. "It came out of nowhere."

"Probably from a lack of sleep." Sue Ellen flashed a

wry grin. "You've got yourself quite a stud there. Mac and I had to take a long walk to cool off."

Her face heated. "Sorry about that."

"No need to apologize. You're young and in love. Only natural."

Was it love?

Rocco made her feel safe. Adored. Like she could tell him anything and he'd understand. But she wasn't ready to trust her feelings or those he claimed to have for her. Not yet.

"Do you have anything for the headache?"

"Get that jar." Sue Ellen pointed to the shelf lined with mason jars. "The willow bark. Put two tablespoons in a cup of hot water. Let it steep. Sip it slowly. By the time you're done drinking it, the headache should be gone."

Mercy went to the shelf and took the jar down. Sue Ellen's gaze was fastened to her. Heading over to the pots and pans, Mercy waited for the older woman's attention to shift. The second it did, she let the jar slip from her hand, shattering on the floor.

"Oh, no." Mercy stared at the mess. "I'm so clumsy and with this headache pounding—"

"It's all right." Sighing, Sue Ellen stood. "Clean it up and then take these sacks of food out to the trucks that they're going to use. I'll run over to Barb's cabin. See if she has any."

"Thank you." Mercy grabbed the broom and dustpan. "Sorry about the hassle."

Sue Ellen trudged outside, and Mercy quickly swept up the debris, tossing it in the trash bin.

She looked out the window. The woman marched

passed the group of men without a glance behind her. Cormac was completely engaged, chatting and laughing with Rocco.

Mercy made a beeline to the Faraday pouch. Velcro buzzed as she opened the bag. She took out the phone and shoved it into the pocket of her sweater. Quickly, she closed it and returned the pouch to the hook the same way she'd found it.

Scooping up the sacks of food, she scurried outside. The four loaded trucks were parked in a row, all facing the gate, ready to leave.

She caught Rocco's eye and gave a curt nod, letting him know that she'd gotten it. Now she just had to slip him the phone without anyone seeing. She hurried to the trucks and set a sack on the console. As she put the last one down, the front gate swung open.

A black SUV pulled in. Shawn was driving.

Worry flooded her nervous system. Why was he there?

Soon enough she'd find out, but whatever the reason, it wasn't good.

Making a U-turn and pulling up beside her, he stopped the vehicle. Cormac and Rocco set down glass bottles and both headed in her direction. She went around to the driver's side.

Shawn hopped out, leaving the car running. "I'm here to bring you back, Mercy."

A jolt shot through her, spurring her to step away from him. "I'm afraid you're wasting your time. I'm not going back to the compound."

He reached into his back pocket, pulled out two envelopes, and handed her one with her name scrawled on the front. Her uncle's name was on the other.

"Read it," Shawn said.

Hurriedly, she tore it open, pulled the handwritten note out and glanced at it.

My dear Mercy,
Come home.
    Or you leave me no choice but to tell your uncle the truth about Rocco.
Empyrean

Her heart twisted, her eyes stinging at the words. Anger built like a pressure wave behind her sternum.

There was no end to his manipulation. To his schemes.

Shawn opened the rear door. "What's it going to be?"

Her breath stalled in her lungs. She wanted to run. She wanted to fight. She wanted to rip the second note to shreds. She wanted to strangle Shawn with her bare hands, preventing him from uttering a word since she wasn't sure how much he knew.

But her father always had a fail-safe.

"Decide. Now." Shawn held up the other envelope, waving it in her face.

Crumbling her note in her hand, she climbed into the car before she lost the nerve to do so. The only thing stronger than her rage was her fear for Rocco.

Precisely what her father had been counting on. As much as she wanted to deny her feelings for Rocco, there was no escaping how much she cared for him.

Shawn closed the door and stuffed the other envelope back in his pocket.

Cormac and Rocco approached them.

She rolled down the window. "I've decided to go back to the compound."

Looking as blindsided as she felt, Rocco shook his head. "What? No."

"Marshall radioed earlier saying he was sending someone up and to keep it a surprise," her uncle said, "but he didn't mention who or for what purpose."

"Empyrean fears for the safety of his daughter," Shawn said. "He got a bad feeling during morning meditation and decided to bring her back for tonight's ceremony."

"Is it safe for her there?" her uncle asked. "I heard about what Alex did to her."

"My father locked him up." But that didn't mean she'd be safe.

"It's for one night. She'll be well protected." Shawn got back inside the SUV. "Rocco, you're welcome to get her tomorrow. Empyrean believed you'd be inclined to stay behind."

He had no choice but to. Her uncle still hadn't told him what the planned target was for the attack. Cormac had decided to wait until they were on the road.

The thought occurred to her that the only reason her father would extend the invitation to Rocco was because he didn't expect him to be able to act on it. Her father didn't think he'd survive.

"Mercy, get out of the car." Rocco grabbed the door handle as Shawn engaged the locks with a *click*.

"I have to go," she said.

"Sure this is what you want, nugget?"

She glanced at her uncle. "I'm positive."

"What's happening?" Rocco reached inside, taking her hand. "What did your father do? Get out and let's speak privately."

His frantic eyes bore into her, their gazes fused.

"She's not leaving the vehicle," Shawn said.

She slipped the crumpled note into his palm, closing his fingers around it. "This is for the best. There's no way around it."

A sick, helpless feeling welled in the pit of her stomach. She was stuck. Staying meant Rocco would be exposed and surely killed. But by leaving, he'd have no one to watch his back.

Had her father foreseen something? Were his visions even real? Or was it all one big con—the puppet master pulling more strings?

A true headache began to pulse in her temples.

"Say goodbye," Shawn said.

Cormac patted Rocco on the back. "I'll give you a minute."

"Whatever the problem is, we can solve it together," Rocco said. "Just get out of the car. You don't have to do this."

"Yes, I do. Believe me." She wouldn't let anything happen to him. Not because of her. "You have to let me go. *Please.*"

Shawn revved the engine.

Rocco leaned in through the window for a slow, thorough kiss that left her tingling all over, and her heart about to split in two. "I'll come for you," he said.

"I know you will." And that was what worried her because her father would assume the same and take steps to prevent it.

He kissed her forehead, his lips lingering and the warmth of his exhalation caressing her skin.

In that moment, with her uncle not watching and Shawn averting his gaze, she took the cell phone from her sweater, reached over, and slipped it into the front pocket of his jeans. "Be safe. Stay alive."

"I love you, Mercy."

Shawn hit the gas, speeding off, tearing them apart before she could respond. Not that she was sure what to say. He rolled up her window and raced through the gate.

She turned around and looked through the rear windshield. Rocco stood there, looking achingly gorgeous. Formidable.

A heavy, burning weight settled in her chest.

He wasn't even out of sight yet, and she missed him already. Being in his arms, with her head on his shoulder, her face pressed to the crook of his neck felt right.

Meant to be.

As if all the times she'd gone into town, looking for something to change, for something that was uniquely hers, for something to spark in her heart, she'd been searching for him.

Not simply a man. Not someone like him, but Rocco.

She hated her father for wanting to take this away from her.

Shawn keyed a radio. "Empyrean. Come in."

A strange fear crept over her.

"Do you have Mercy?" her father asked, making her temples throb and her breath grow shallow.

"I do."

A tingling sensation spread through her arms down

to her fingers. Her heart raced, each beat pounding through her.

"Good. Hurry home."

Facing forward, she tried to swallow the bitter dread rising in her throat at what her father had planned for her at the compound.

The sense of impending doom wormed through her veins, tightening in her chest, blurring her vision.

What was happening to her? Was it another anxiety attack? It was nothing like her allergic reaction, but she still felt like she was dying.

Panic washed over her in a cold, blistering wave, and all she could do was roll down the window, letting the fresh air rush over her, close her eyes and pray.

Chapter Seventeen

Two hours.

Mercy had been gone only two hours, and it felt like a lifetime.

Rocco was split down the middle, a war raging inside his heart as he rode in one of the trucks. He would've done anything to stop her from leaving…if he didn't have a job to do. If lives weren't hanging in the balance.

After reading the note, he understood. Her father's trap. Her choice to save him.

Fury was a noose strangling him.

Any minute, she'd be back at the compound, if she wasn't there already. What was going to happen to her then?

The uncertainty had unease slithering through his veins.

At least Alex would be locked up, unable to hurt her again.

He tightened his grip on the AK-47 in his hands. He'd been given the weapon along with a bulletproof vest that would protect the Brotherhood from shots fired by law enforcement. But it wouldn't protect Rocco from their armor-piercing rounds.

Their vehicle hit a pothole, jostling them. They'd left about thirty minutes after Mercy and were almost out of the mountains. He was in the back seat of the lead truck—the black dually that had run Dr. Percy Tiggs off the road. Rocco was sitting beside Barry—a man who smelled like he'd been sleeping outdoors for one too many nights without a shower. Mac was in the passenger's seat and behind the wheel, in front of Rocco, was Dennis.

Although Rocco had an assault rifle, the two up front also carried backup 9 mms while Barry had a Calico M950 submachine gun slung over his right shoulder and a bowie knife holstered on his left hip.

Rocco gave a furtive glance down at the knife on Barry's hip beside him. "I heard about how you two took care of a federal informant."

"Sure did," Dennis said with a nod. "Barry shot him, and I ran him off the road."

"That's what I'm talking about." Rocco patted Barry's shoulder. "Wish I had been given the chance to do the same to the ATF agent who wormed his way into the compound."

"Don't worry. That one might've gotten away, but you're about to have a much sweeter opportunity."

"So, where are we headed?" Rocco asked. "The not knowing is driving me nuts."

"All right. You've earned the right to know." Mac drummed his fingers on the dashboard. "We are going to hit the main headquarters for the ATF," he said, and Barry howled. "Federal building in the capital. If we're lucky we might take out some secret service, too."

Rocco's gut clenched.

Not only was the ATF and secret service in that federal building, but the US district court as well. The building was made of reinforced concrete, spanned almost two acres, and had guards. It wasn't a quick and simple target, but it was teeming with people. More than two hundred federal employees worked inside, and countless civilians passed by there every day.

"That's a big, fortified site, isn't it?" Rocco asked. "Maybe we should pick a smaller target. Easy pickings, you know. Molotov cocktails won't do much there."

"Don't get your panties in a bunch." The horse guy gave his arm a playful punch, and Dennis laughed.

"I've got an inside person working in the building," Mac said. "Security guard who has been there about a year. We've worked it out. He's going to pull the fire alarm once I give him the signal. As everybody pours out of the building, milling around, we'll strike. The site is large, taking up an entire square block. That's why we've got four vehicles to cover all the exits. I promised you blood in the streets and I always keep my word."

MARSHALL STOOD IN the foyer as Shawn hauled his daughter inside the house. Mercy glared at him, seething and silent. They both removed their shoes, and Shawn brought her up to him.

Clasping his hands behind his back, Marshall gave her a sympathetic smile.

She looked ready to spit in his face, but then schooled her features. Standing with a sense of grace and decorum that belied her anger, she now appeared so composed, so poised that he might have believed this was any other day.

Except that her hands trembled ever so slightly.

"We will speak later, my dear, and all will be made clear," he said to her. Marshall looked at Shawn. "Take her up to her room. Lock her inside." He handed him the padlock and key.

She thought she hated him, but his work wasn't finished yet. After this was all said and done, what she was feeling now would only scratch the surface.

Marshall watched them ascend the stairs and returned to his office. He'd broken her heart, wounded her deeply in his actions. This did not please him. He found no joy in her pain.

Now that Mercy was safe under his roof and locked away in her room, Marshall picked up the radio. Once Rocco was dead and she had no one else to turn to on the outside, she would finally fall into line. Take her vows.

The commune, this family, would help her heal. The memory of Rocco would fade in time.

And she would find true happiness in the Light.

If she never forgave Marshall for what he was about to do, so be it. Defining relationships and responding to them with exactly what was needed was one of his greatest skills. He would make the same choice again, sacrificing her love for him, to save her soul from darkness.

But Rocco had to die for this to work.

Everything Marshall was doing was necessary. This was his responsibility as father. As prophet. As Empyrean.

Heavy is the head that wears the crown.

STARING OUT THE window at the trees rushing by, Rocco struggled to come up with a way out of this. To his left was an escarpment, a slope falling at least two hundred feet. No guardrail, only a precipitous drop with trees along this stretch of road. To his right was the rocky, equally steep mountainside.

A bad place to ask them to pull over so he could answer nature's call.

In a few more minutes, they'd pass Wayward Bluffs and clear the mountains. Just before they hit the interstate, he'd get them to make a pit stop. Blame it on nerves or a weak bladder. Anything to give him a chance to get a message to Nash so he could warn the folks at the federal building.

The radio up front squawked. "Mac. Are you there?" Marshall's anxious voice crackled over the static.

Rocco's heart squeezed, a flurry of worries whirling in his head.

Was Mercy okay? Had something happened to her?

He met Mac's gaze in the rearview mirror, a thought suddenly niggling his mind. What if Marshall wasn't calling about Mercy?

What if it was about him?

Only a blind fool would think her father incapable of a double cross. But if things kicked off in the cabin of the truck it would not bode well for Rocco. All he had was a long assault rifle. Trying to fire it in a confined space that required close-quarters combat would prove disastrous.

Not to mention there were three more trucks of heavily armed men right behind them.

Mercy's uncle grabbed the radio from the dash and hit the button on the side. "I'm here, Marsh. Go ahead."

"I just found out. I'm in shock, ashamed, at having been fooled," Marshall said in a rush. "But we've all been deceived."

A prickle of warning crawled up Rocco's neck. He tensed, his muscles coiling with readiness.

"What on earth?" Mac leaned forward, hunching over the radio. "Deceived about what?"

"Not what, my brother, but by *who*. Rocco is an undercover ATF agent. I trust you to handle it as you see fit."

Rocco's chest constricted, his adrenaline kicking into high gear.

Nanoseconds bled together. Everything happened in slow motion. Barry turned for him. At the same time, Rocco raised the AK-47 and slammed the butt of the rifle into the man's face.

Bone crunched. Blood gushed.

Mac was in motion, shifting in his seat.

Rocco swung the buttstock ninety degrees. Smashed it forward between the front seats against the side of Mac's head, sending his skull crashing into the window.

The truck swerved as Dennis reached for a weapon. Rocco ignored him. Only the other two men mattered at the moment.

With his right hand, Rocco snatched the bowie knife from Barry's holster. He rotated his elbow up and jammed the blade back into the man's throat.

A wet gurgling came from Barry.

Rocco yanked the knife free. Barry's hand, now gripping the wound, was so coated in blood it seemed as though he had slipped on a crimson glove.

Almost too late, he caught sight of Mac grabbing a 9 mm. *Almost.* Rocco pounced forward. A bullet rifled by him—close enough that he felt the heat at the side of his neck—shattering the rear windshield. He thrust the bowie knife into flesh, sinking the sharp blade into Mac's wrist.

The 9 mm clattered to the footwell.

Rocco grabbed the strap of his seat belt, wrapping the webbing around his left arm. Lunging up, he pressed the button on the buckle for Dennis, releasing the driver's safety belt. He punched Dennis in the temple with a hammer fist, using the fleshy side part of his clenched hand.

Then he grabbed the steering wheel and yanked it hard, pitching them off the road and down the steep hillside.

His heart whipped up into his throat. His stomach dropped. The saliva dried in his mouth. Bracing, he tightened his grip on the seat belt webbing that locked in place.

A string of curses flew from Mac's mouth. The man tried to wrangle the steering wheel with his one good hand, but it was no use. The truck was out of control.

The heavy dually whooshed down the slope. Angry metal chewed through brush, barreling over shrubs. Nausea welled in Rocco. A burst of fear slicing through him was razor sharp.

Fear that he would fail to stop the other men from launching the attack. That he wouldn't keep his promise to get Mercy out of the compound.

The groan of steel crunching and rending filled his

ears when the passenger's side of the truck wrapped around a tree, bringing them to a bone-jarring halt. The sudden impact had him lurching forward, but the safety belt he clung to jerked tight, snapping him back against the seat.

His brain felt like it had been caught in a blender. His stomach in a knot. His left shoulder ached from the force of the impact.

Clearing his head, he gained his bearings.

Barry was dead, bled out beside him. Mac was unconscious with a deployed airbag in his face.

But Dennis was gone. His body had been thrown from the vehicle, out through the windshield.

Rocco looked around. Found the Calico submachine gun and the 9 mm Mac had dropped in the footwell. He grabbed both.

He pulled on the handle of his door. It stuck. He had to kick it open.

Glancing back at Mac, he ached to put a bullet in him, sending his soul straight to hell. He had to remind himself that he wasn't a vigilante doling out his own brand of justice.

Self-defense was one thing, but taking the life of an unconscious man wasn't how he operated. Not now. Not ever.

He shoved out of the truck. The air was dank and thick with the smell of gasoline from the shattered Molotov cocktails that had been in the back. But there were plenty more in the other trucks.

Shouts and hollering came from the hillside above. Voices and footfalls were moving downhill. Mac's men were racing to help him. They were drawing nearer. Getting close. Too darned close, way too fast.

On a surge of adrenaline, he cut through the trees, moving laterally, away from the crash. He stuffed the 9 mm in the back of his waistband and kept hold of the submachine gun.

His heart hammered. With each frantic, hurried step he took, he cursed Marshall McCoy and the depth of his betrayal.

Once he made it several yards west, he veered north. Going uphill. Circling back toward the vehicles that had stopped to help.

Branches slapped his face. He climbed upward. Shoving off trees for leverage. He licked his lips in desperation. *Faster.* He needed to move faster. Sweat ran down his spine. His shoulder hurt like hell. The air was thin, and his lungs were on fire.

Hurry, hurry!

He scrabbled up the hillside. Running. Trying to stay low in the trees, to keep his footsteps stealthy as he hurried. Determination propelled him forward.

Drawing close to the road above him, he stopped and strained to listen. At first there was only the pounding of his heartbeat like a drum in his ears. He swiped at the moisture in his eyes and drew in a long, calming breath.

There.

The scuffle of boots on asphalt. Two voices.

Concentrate. Focus. He needed to be sure.

A third person coughed. There were three men. One had probably stayed behind with each truck.

He crept up higher to a tree just off the road and rolled across the back of the trunk, taking a position where he could see them. Standing at an angle, his bladed body presenting a narrower target, he peeked out.

They were farther back on the road. All three men were peering over the edge, their focus on the wreckage down the hill.

Rocco had gauged correctly and was only a few feet from the front bumper of the first truck. But he'd never make it to the door, much less inside the vehicle before they spotted him.

A bullet bit into the tree trunk near his head, forcing him to duck. The gunfire had come from downhill. Some of the guys must have tracked him.

He rolled out from behind the tree, taking aim at the men on the road as he rose onto a knee.

A quick squeeze on the hairpin trigger. Four bullets popped off with a *rat-a-tat-tat*.

Two men dropped, screaming and clutching their thighs. The third one managed to sidestep out of sight.

Rocco aimed for the tires of the second truck. Fired a shot, flattening the front tire. He did the same with the third vehicle. Squeezing off more rounds to force the third guy to stay concealed, he bolted for the driver's side door and hopped in the truck.

In their haste to help Cormac, they'd left the keys in the ignition with the engine running. He threw the gear in Drive and sped off.

Gunshots rang out behind him. He prayed none would hit any of the explosives in the back.

Pop! Pop!

The rear windshield exploded. Rocco flinched, lowering his head. Flooring the gas, he took the bend in the road as fast as he dared.

He flicked a glance in the rearview mirror. All clear. But he didn't ease off the accelerator. He pulled the cell phone from his pocket, turned it on, and waited for it to power up.

As soon as he got a signal, he called Nash Garner and told him everything.

Chapter Eighteen

The padlock outside her bedroom door rattled. The shackle clicked, unhinging and metal clanged as the lock was removed from the hasp.

Wearing the same clothes that she'd arrived in, blue jeans, a T-shirt and gray sweater, Mercy stood. She steeled herself to face her father.

No matter what he said, she was done with the Shining Light. She was leaving after Rocco's mission. Today. As one of the fallen.

She'd deal with the implications to her soul once she was free of Empyrean.

The door swung open, and Alex stepped inside.

Her heart clutched.

He shut it behind him, bent down and shoved a door stop tight under the lip.

Mercy's blood turned to ice. In the time it would take for her to remove the wedge and open the door to get out, she would be at a distinct disadvantage, and he would be on top of her. "Why aren't you locked up?"

Alex pressed a palm to the door and leaned against it. His eyes had a weird, glassy look to them. "I atoned and father released me," he said, his words slurring. Like he was drunk. Or high.

Which was odd. Alex didn't drink and he didn't do drugs. He only did ayahuasca once for his shedding ceremony.

"How did you get the key to get in here?"

He grinned. "I have my ways."

Alex must have coerced Shawn to give him the key.

Biting her lip, she forced herself not to panic. "What's wrong with you?"

He chuckled. "There are so many things, I don't know where to start."

Alex was on something. But why?

"When you look at me, what do you see?" he asked. "Be honest."

A pathetic, petty, green-eyed… "A monster."

He gave a sad laugh that tugged at her heartstrings, despite telling herself not to care about him. "You'll never marry me, will you? Not after the chili."

Trying to kill her was the point of no return. Not what put her off as a potential partner. He was delusional. Deranged.

Squeezing her eyes shut for the span of a breath, she hoped he didn't have a gun tucked at the small of his back with plans to put a bullet in her head.

"Why would you want to marry me when you know I don't love you?" she asked.

"Because I love you enough for both of us. I'd do anything for you."

She looked at him. "Even let me go?"

Smirking, he wagged a finger. "True love requires conviction." He shoved off the door and stalked toward her.

"True love requires compassion. Kindness. Neither of which you showed me when you tried to kill me." She stood her ground, clenching her hands into fists.

He grasped a handful of her hair, gently, and put the strands to his nose. Inhaled deeply. "I always thought we'd save ourselves for our wedding night. But then you gave away your purity to that man. I feel cheated."

Her skin crawled.

"How about you give me a taste of what you gave him, huh?" He leaned in to kiss her.

She wasn't a violent person. She wasn't even a fighter. But Rocco had taught her that raw, desperate fury in a strong body should never be discounted.

Because it was powerful.

Mercy rammed her knee up into his unprotected groin. She felt the softness there and knew she'd made contact when he cried out and hunched over. But she didn't stop. She shoved him away.

He staggered back, trying to recover. As soon as he straightened, she punched his chest, striking the spot Rocco called the solar plexus. He'd told her when you got the blow right it caused momentary paralysis of the diaphragm, making it difficult to breathe.

The force of the punch, or more likely the shock, knocked Alex off his feet. His back hit the floor and he flailed like he was being electrocuted. Gasping and thrashing, he rolled onto his side. His face was wrenched in agony.

She never wanted anyone to suffer. Her instinct was to help him. But she ran to the door. Pulled out the wedge and tossed it to the side.

"Wait," he wheezed, gasping for breath, looking weak and pained. "Help. Me."

Mercy stared at him. Frozen. Unsure what to do.

He rolled onto his hands and knees. Bloody spots bloomed on the back of his gray shirt.

Her feet were moving before she thought to act. She grabbed his outstretched hand and got him up onto her bed. Helping him was a force of habit.

He lay down on his side, curling up in a ball.

"What happened to you?" she asked.

He unbuttoned his shirt and showed her his back that was covered in gauze soaked with blood. "Flagellation."

"You took something strong for the pain?"

With those glazed eyes, he nodded.

"Alex, I have to leave. I can't stay here any longer."

Tears fell from his eyes. "I know. Because of me."

This was so much bigger than him. "I was never meant to be a Starlight." She let his hand go and inched away to the door.

"Do you remember my favorite book?" he asked, stopping her. "When we were younger."

How could she ever forget. "*Frankenstein* by Mary Shelley. You read it ten times."

"Everyone thinks the Creature is the monster. He was just misunderstood. And lonely. But Victor Frankenstein, the one who made the Creature—he was the real monster. Why doesn't anyone see it?" A sob broke through him, and he cried. "I've become a monster, too. But I'm what our father made me. I only did to you what he did to Ayanna. And yet, his princess still loves him."

"What?" She went to his side and lowered to her knees.

"The allergic reaction."

"He put peanuts in my mother's food?"

Alex nodded. "I watched him do it. He didn't know I was there in the kitchen. He even made sure the doctor was close by to save her. That's how I got the idea."

A hot flash of rage tangled with the sorrow rising in her chest. "How could I be so blind to who he is?"

"He worked very hard to blind you. And I helped him do it."

She was on her feet, headed for the door.

"Mercy. Please," he begged, "don't leave me. I need you!"

With hot tears welling in her eyes, she flew out the door. Ran down the steps. Grabbed her shoes. Reached for the handle of the front door.

A squawk from a radio made her still.

"Marsh, pick up." Her uncle Cormac's voice carried through the house.

She spun around and crept down the hall toward her father's office.

"Pick. Up," Cormac demanded.

Passing the mural of the Shining Light's symbol on the wall, she looked around for any guards. There were none lurking.

"I know you can hear me, Marsh. Pick up, you son of a—"

Static cut through the line. "I'm here, Mac," her father said. "Did you take care of our little problem?"

She stopped outside his office and peered in through the open door.

Her father strode to a window with the radio in his hand.

"You didn't tell me everything," Mac said.

"What do you mean? Of course, I did."

"Rocco is more than an ATF agent."

Her heart seized. Mac knew the truth. Rocco was in danger.

"Was he Special Forces?" Cormac asked "SWAT? What the hell is he? A former assassin?"

"I have no idea." Her father sounded confused, over-whelmed, two things he never was. "I told you every-thing I know as soon as I learned it," he said, and she tipped her head back against the onslaught of pain at yet another of her father's betrayals. "Does this mean he got away?"

"Yeah, he got away. He's more slippery than a prai-rie rattlesnake. Deadlier, too. He killed two of my guys. Wounded me and two others before he escaped."

Praise be. Relief flooded her. She thanked the Light.

"It was a mistake to hesitate," her father said. "You should've dealt with him immediately."

"The mistake was yours, sending an undercover agent into my camp." Her uncle's anger radiated over the wireless.

"I'm sure there are things you'd like to further *dis-cuss* with him. His task force has an office here in town." Her father gave him an address on Second Street. "Ground floor. Perhaps this time more preparedness is required."

How did he know where their office was located? Did he have Nash and Becca followed after they left?

"We'll take care of Rocco," Cormac promised. "Then we're coming to the compound for you and Mercy."

She tensed, thinking about the hundreds of innocent Starlights that had nothing to do with this.

"As I've stated, I only just learned the truth. Mercy was devastated to hear her intended was a deceitful Fed." The radio chirped. "Mac?" Her father pressed the button on the radio several times. "Cormac?"

"What have you done?" Mercy asked, storming into his office.

Her father spun on his heels. "My dear, what are you doing out of your room, scurrying around the halls, like a rat?"

"You disgust me. How could you betray Rocco after I came back like you wanted?"

He set the radio down. "If that man lives, you will leave again. But if he dies—"

"I would hate you forever."

"A price I'm willing to pay, so long as you stay where you belong."

Mercy shook her head in disbelief. "You made an agreement in good faith with Agents Garner and Hammond and Rocco."

"I signed no papers. Gave no oaths. My only obligation is to this commune and the Shining Light."

"To the Light?" Mercy barked a harsh laugh. "All you know is darkness. You knew what Cormac was planning all along. Didn't you?"

"Not the specifics. That would make me culpable. My hands are clean regarding anything the Brotherhood does."

Her stomach pulled into a tight, hard knot. "Naturally, you'd want plausible deniability, but you were aware that people were going to die today as a result of whatever he was going to do and you had no intention of stopping it."

"I am not my brother's keeper." Sighing, he half sat, half leaned on the edge of his desk. "Besides, why would I stop it? Every time there is chaos and death in the streets our numbers increase. Your uncle has gotten far more active in the last five years and the number of my followers have grown tremendously as a result. I welcome his actions. He is doing me a service."

Everything her father was saying made her furious and queasy at the same time. "I once believed in you and what you preached. Then you tried to kill my mother and forced her to leave me behind. That's when it all changed for me." She studied his face, looking for a drop of remorse. Waited for him to explain, even though it would only be more lies.

Clasping his hands, he nodded, slowly, soberly. "Alex let you out and told you. If he can't have your love, I suppose he doesn't want me to either."

"Aren't you even going to deny it?"

"Would you believe me if I tried?" He stood and moved toward her, but she backed away. "This reminds me of that part in the *Wizard of Oz* when Dorothy sees behind the curtain."

The Great Empyrean was smoke and mirrors. A fraud.

"How could you do that my mother?" she asked. "To me? Separate us like that."

"I did what was necessary. Even though it was hard. To protect you."

"You've never protected me. All you've ever done is manipulate and coerce me to follow your will. Now you want to kill Rocco. Why? Because you think he's going to take me away? Because he loves me?" Saying the words, she felt them to be true.

Rocco did love her. He'd been nothing but compassionate, kind and caring. And she loved him, too. She'd sacrifice anything to keep him safe. Even her own happiness. In her heart, she believed he'd do the same for her.

Mercy stared at her father. A mix of anger and anguish filled her heaving chest. "You're *evil.*"

"Evil? No, no, my dear." The great Empyrean threw his arms out to his sides with flourish. He approached her with an air of dignity and grace as though he were more than a man walking on water, but she stayed out of his reach because she now saw the truth. "I am no more evil than a hurricane, an earthquake, fire or flood. All serve a purpose that is not easily understood. Underwriters classify those as acts of God."

She reared back. "You are not *vis major.* To even insinuate such a thing only goes to show how polluted your soul has become. He was right about you," she said, thinking of Alex. "You're the real monster. I was just too naive to see it."

"Mercy, everything I've done has been to keep you safe."

"Stop saying that. Everything you've done has been to protect your power and your status. Not me." She wrapped her fingers around the Shining Light necklace that she wore and yanked it off. "I'm done. With you. And this place." She tossed the pendant at his feet.

"Rocco might not survive. If he doesn't, you'll need us." His tone was gentle and coaxing, sickening her.

"You'll need me. Stay the night, my dear. Wait to see what happens before you decide."

She steeled her spine. "My mother left this place with nothing but the clothes on her back and she made it without you. So will I."

"I put you on a pedestal, ensured you were revered above all but me. And the thanks you give me is to throw it away because you want to roll around in the muck and mire with that pig." He narrowed his eyes, his composure slipping away like a discarded mask. "If you leave like this, you will be considered one of the fallen. Banished from the Light. Shunned for the rest of your days."

Her throat closed. She was leaving the only home she'd ever known. People she loved. Everything that was familiar. A movement she had once had complete faith in.

But she had to get far away from Alex. And from the suffocating hold of Marshall McCoy.

"Just like my mother," she said and headed to the door. At the threshold, a whisper of warning made her look back at him. "If you do anything to prevent me from leaving, pull some stunt, I will tell any acolyte willing to listen who you really are. The devil. And they'll believe every word from my mouth. Let me go and I wash my hands of you and the commune in every way."

He was quiet for a moment, thinking, plotting, ever scheming. "You'll say nothing of the things you've overheard?"

Disappointment seared through her. They were talking about her life, her safety, and he was bargaining for his reputation. "No. Not a word."

Even if she did, her father had a remarkable knack for wiggling out of trouble. None of Cormac's despicable deeds would stick to him.

"You may doubt me, but I love you and have only worked for your highest good. If you're certain you wish to leave…so shall it be." He picked up the phone and pressed a button. "Mercy is on her way down to the gate. She is not to be given a ride, but you are to let her out. Then we're going on lockdown. No one else in or out of the compound. Security is to be tripled. A credible threat has been made against us." He pressed down on the receiver and then dialed a number, three digits. After a moment, he said, "I'd like to report a potential attack on the office of a federal task force on Second Street."

That was just like her father. Covering his bases. Protecting himself above everyone else.

Mercy rushed to the front door and put on her shoes. She ran down the steps and the hill. Her lungs opened and it was as if a massive weight had lifted from her, but Rocco and the task force were still in danger.

The guard spotted her. He waved. The front gate swung open.

"I need to use the phone," she said, breathless, and pointed to the one in the guardhouse.

"I was only told to let you out."

"My father said I wasn't to be given a ride. He said nothing about me using the phone."

Uncertainty crossed his face, but he stepped aside. "Hit nine for an outside line."

She moved past him and picked up the phone. After she pressed nine, she realized she knew just one phone number and dialed it.

"Hello, this is the Underground Self-Defense school. How can I help you?"

"Charlie," Mercy said, her pulse pounding. "Rocco, Brian, the entire task force is in danger." She hoped her father had called the police, but she knew better than to trust him.

"Slow down. Where are you?"

"Outside the gates of the compound. I'm heading to town. On foot."

"I'll come get you."

"First, you have to help them. They need to evacuate the office on Second Street. Call the police. And the sheriff." Was there time to mobilize the national guard? "The state police, too. Let them know that the Brotherhood of the Silver Light is on the way. They're radical, dangerous and heavily armed with guns and explosives."

Chapter Nineteen

Finally, back in town, Rocco sped down the road up to the meeting spot. Nash had called him back with an update. The FBI's CIRG—Critical Incident Response Group—were mobilizing to raid Cormac's camp and seize the cache of weapons. SWAT had secured the federal building in Cheyenne and authorities were searching for Cormac's insider. But their target had changed. The Brotherhood planned to launch an attack in town.

Now the Laramie PD, sheriff's department and state highway patrol were gathered at Cottonwood Park, conferring on how to handle the Brotherhood. Rocco had expected Cormac to alter his plan, but he hadn't counted on him waging war in town.

He pulled up to the park. Wearing a bulletproof vest, Brian waved him past two officers standing by police cruisers.

Rocco stopped near a long row of law-enforcement vehicles and got out.

Brian was looking through the arsenal loaded in the back. "Two more trucks like this are coming?"

"Yeah, and they won't be far behind. Fifteen, maybe twenty minutes."

"They're finalizing the plan now," Brian said, hiking his chin at the huddle of law-enforcement officers. "All the businesses in our section of Second Street have been evacuated. Thanks to Mercy, we had a good idea of what to expect."

"Where is she?" The words grated painfully against his throat. If she was still trapped on that compound and had only managed to get out a message, he was going to lose it. There'd be no way for him to focus on the task at hand—putting a stop to the Brotherhood.

"Rocco!"

The sound of Mercy's voice had him spinning around. The sight of her running to him burrowed into an empty place in his heart, filling it with warmth.

She flew into his outstretched arms or he into hers. All he knew was that he was holding her tight.

"Don't ever leave me like that." He kissed the crown of her head and squeezed her tighter. "Don't leave me at all."

"Think you're stuck with me," she said between quick, shallow breaths.

That was fine by him. "I love you so much."

"Love you, too."

He put her down and stared into those blue, blue eyes. "Say that again."

She pressed a palm to his cheek. "I love you, Rocco. I was afraid of how I felt, of whether to trust your feelings for me, but not anymore. I'm out of the movement. Done with my father."

With his fingers, he brushed the hollow of her throat where the Shining Light pendant used to rest. He was pleased she'd taken it off and relieved she'd finally gotten free of her father.

"Sorry to break up this reunion," Nash said, standing with several others who had been watching them. "But we've got domestic terrorists to stop."

Rocco looked over the group: Sheriff Daniel Clark, Chief of Police Willa Nelson, Becca, Charlie, Chief Deputy Holden Powell and his brother, state trooper Monty Powell. They had quite the audience.

"I flattened a couple of their tires," Rocco said, "but it won't take them long to change them."

"We've got highway patrol on the lookout for them. The plan is to trap Cormac McCoy and his men on Second Street, where it's clear of civilians," Nash said. "We've put out the warning for folks to get inside, stay off the streets, and we're positioning some plain-clothes officers. We'll funnel them in, helping them get to where they think they want to go. Then we'll block off Second Street with LPD on one end and the sheriff's department on the other."

A solid plan. They had to be smart about this. No room for mistakes. With the Brotherhood using armor-piercing bullets they couldn't approach this situation as they might under normal circumstances.

"What about us?" Rocco asked.

"You, me, Brian and the state troopers will take positions on the rooftops. Everyone is aware that they're using armor-piercing ammo. If they open fire, we shoot to kill."

IN A DPO—discontinued post office—the task force had previously requisitioned as a backup headquarters, Mercy stood beside the chair Charlie sat in. She was too nervous to sit. Becca was seated across the table along with an LPD officer.

The DPO was located on a side street that intersected Second, right around the corner from the task force's primary office. Mercy stared at the three law-enforcement vehicles, including an armored tank, parked outside, positioned at the ready to block off Second Street once the Brotherhood had entered the trap.

"They're here, just got off Highway 130," a patrol officer said over the radio that was on the table. "Four men inside each vehicle along with four more sitting in the truck beds, holding assault rifles. Sixteen gunmen total. Both vehicles are now turning onto Snowy Range Road."

"So far, they're taking the route we expected," Becca said, her gaze bouncing between Mercy and Charlie. "We've also closed off certain streets to prevent a detour."

Mercy wrung her hands, trying not to worry, but it was impossible.

"It's going to be okay," Charlie said low to her. "They've got this. None of the good guys out there will let any civilians get hurt."

But what about the good guys getting hurt?

"They just turned onto Second," the trooper said. "Ten blocks away. Looks like a ghost town with no one on the street. So far they don't seem suspicious. Still headed in your direction. Going the speed limit. Nine blocks."

Fear coursed through Mercy, her mind racing. Rocco had to be all right. Brian, Nash, all the officers who were putting their lives on the line to protect the town needed to be safe.

They just had to be.

"Seven blocks," the patrol officer said. "Six. They're stopping at a red light. I'm hanging back."

The authorities were armed and well-trained, but their tactical gear wouldn't protect them. Not from armor-piercing rounds that would tear through their vests like a hot knife through butter. At least officers on the ground had a tank to hide behind.

But those positioned on the rooftops would be partially exposed.

"Five." The tension in the patrol officer's voice vibrated through her. "Four."

"We've got a visual," Nash said. "Got them in our sights."

Seconds crawled by. With each one, Mercy forced herself to take deep, steady breaths and not panic. It wouldn't do anyone any good, least of all Rocco.

"Three blocks...two...you're a go."

The vehicles outside, with the armored tank leading the way, sped into position.

Mercy ran to the window and looked down the street. She could see where the officers stopped, blocking off that end of Second Street. But then her stress skyrocketed with the next sound.

The assault kicked off without warning.

A single shot became a raging torrent of gunfire faster than the ear could comprehend. Automatic weapons spit out a barrage of bullets.

She hated not knowing what was happening. The only thing certain was that this was risky. Dangerous for anyone going up against her uncle and his people.

"Officer down," someone said over the radio.

Terror rushed over Mercy now in a hot, stifling wave. It took every ounce of willpower for her to stay put. Who had been shot?

"Would they use the term 'officer' to refer to any law-enforcement person?" Mercy asked.

With a grim expression, Becca nodded. "Yes, they would."

Her first thought was Rocco. Lying in a prone position on the roof, if he got hit, it would be to the head. Was he okay?

Pacing in front of the window, she interlaced her fingers and prayed. To the Light. To the universe. To any higher power that would hear and answer, to let everyone make it through.

"Another officer down," a female voice said. "Officer down."

Ka-BOOM!

An explosion thundered, making Mercy jump as she looked outside. It was deafening. A tower of flames, smoke and debris shot up into the air past the clearance of the two-story building.

"Oh, no." The words slipped from her lips as every muscle tensed.

There were two more gunshots. Then nothing.

Mercy released the breath she'd been holding and opened her eyes when the gunfire stopped.

It was quiet.

With guns raised, the officers she could see down the street moved from behind their vehicles and rushed down the street out of view.

Was it over?

Who was hurt? Or worse, who had been killed?

The fear and adrenaline rubbed her nerves raw.

"We need an ambulance," someone said over the radio. "Deputy Holden Powell was shot in the shoulder. He's going to be okay. But Officer Tyson…he didn't make it."

No, no, no.

Mercy covered her mouth with her hand. She'd never met Officer Tyson, but he was someone's son, possibly a brother or husband. There were people who loved him, who'd miss him. Who would grieve his death.

"We've got Cormac McCoy and two of his men in custody," Nash said. "The rest are dead."

So many senseless deaths. And for what?

In the distance, Mercy heard the wail of the ambulance that had been on standby. Since it was coming from just three blocks over, it wouldn't take long to get there.

Rocco rounded the corner. Alive and unharmed. Headed her way, taking those long, powerful strides. Relief thrust her breath from her lungs in a long sigh even though she already knew he hadn't been injured. Seeing him made it real.

He'd done it—he and this team made sure that the Brotherhood wouldn't hurt anyone else ever again.

Four days later

ROCCO COULDN'T BELIEVE his good fortune. He had one month of use or lose vacation days that Nash had ordered him to take after they wrapped up the case with the Brotherhood of the Silver Light.

During the FBI's CIRG raid on Cormac's camp, all

members of the Brotherhood were arrested and taken into custody without any injury to law enforcement. The weapons were seized.

Unfortunately, the task force couldn't make any charges stick to Marshall McCoy. His lawyer used the call he'd made to 911 reporting Cormac's intention to help his client slither out of trouble. Rocco wanted Alex arrested for the attempted murder of Mercy, but the district attorney was only willing to go with aggravated assault. When the task force went to arrest Alex, he'd conveniently disappeared.

Rocco suspected it had been through the tunnel in the basement. As long as Alex was on the run, out of town, Rocco would take it as a win.

"I'm glad you're on vacation," Mercy said with a smile as they put away equipment inside the Underground Self-Defense school. She wore simple workout clothes, but looked like a knockout in the pink tank top and navy leggings that clung to her sensational curves.

"Me, too." He had decided to spend the time with the woman who'd captured his heart. They were going to fix up his ranch and create a business plan for Mercy to open a holistic wellness shop, selling candles, soap, bath oils, crystals, legal medicinal herbs and honey. Buying a bee apiary was a feasible and affordable way to start. Bees first. Horses down the line. Putting the idea of opening a shop into action would probably take a year, after scrimping and saving, but he thought it was essential for her to have an actionable plan she was excited about to focus on during her transition. "But somehow working at USD doesn't feel like a vacation."

Mercy chuckled as she bopped to the beat of the

music playing—a pop song on the radio. "You're a good cousin. Charlie works too much. She needs this down time with Brian."

Yes, she did. The woman didn't understand what a lazy day was, but Brian would show her.

"And you're a good girlfriend for helping me."

"I need something constructive to do until my job at Delgado's as a waitress starts," she said. "Besides, spending the time with you is no hardship."

Even though she had the keys to Charlie's place, where she could stay whenever she wanted time to herself since Brian and Charlie were officially cohabitating, so far, Mercy had been spending the nights at his ranch.

He was grateful for every second he got to be with her and couldn't wait for his parents to meet her. They were flying in for Mercy's surprise birthday party next month.

Rocco had the works planned. A live DJ booked, a custom cake and a special guest of honor. Mercy's mother, Ayanna.

The two had connected thanks to Becca tracking down her mom. Reuniting had been healing, transformative for both women. But they hadn't seen each other yet in an environment that was carefree and all about having fun.

He desperately wanted to give Mercy that gift if it was in his power.

Along with his coworkers, the sheriff's department, the LPD and local state troopers were invited to the party. Pretty much half of the town was coming. Mercy might not have the commune, but Rocco was doing everything he could to give her a family. Not one based on vows to the Shining Light, but stronger and more reliable because it was rooted in goodness, basic values and it was comprised of people who all believed in service and self-sacrifice.

He ached to share the details with her, and this was the toughest good secret he'd ever kept.

"I'll dump the trash and load these dirty towels into the car for us to drop off at the cleaners, then we'll lock up and go," he said.

"Okay, I'll shut down the computer."

He grabbed the trash with one hand and the laundry with the other and headed for the back door.

BITING HER LOWER LIP, Mercy watched Rocco walk away and thought about all the things she wanted to do to him later in bed. And what she wanted him to do to her. Experimenting and exploring had been fun. But last night, he'd held her, with no clothes between them, their gazes locked, and time seemed to halt. They stared into each other's eyes, connecting on a level of intimacy that made her heart expand, swelling impossibly big as a balloon in her chest. It was the way he looked at her. Like he wanted her to see his soul, what she meant to him, how much that physical moment affected him.

She wanted lots more of that, too.

A shiver of anticipation ran through her. She shut off the lights in the private training rooms and danced her way to the office, happy to help out. Escaping the jaws of her father's lies and machinations had required more grit and determination than she could have ever imagined. No way could she have done it without Rocco and Charlie. Their support had been unwavering.

She owed them both more than she could ever repay.

Grabbing her purse, she slung it over her head across her body. It was strange having a handbag. But a good kind of strange like everything else she'd tried.

The cherry-red purse and small matching wallet were thoughtful gifts from Charlie, sustainable and vegan. She'd never had one before since there hadn't been a need. But now she had things to carry around. A state-issued ID. Soon a license, since she was learning how to drive. Money—though it was given and not yet earned. In time a bank card. Lip gloss. A cell phone. And Rocco's gift, a SIG Sauer P220 pistol.

She turned off the computer and the radio. Stepping around the desk to hit the lights, she froze.

Alex stood inside USD in front of the office. Her gaze fell to the gun in his hand. Her heart nosedived. His eyes burned with a white-hot rage that sent a different kind of shiver up her spine.

Then a calmness stole over her. Mercy had never been afraid to die. She believed in an afterlife and a paradise for good souls. Even if it wasn't as her father had described, deep down a part of her was still invested in that idea.

But she wasn't ready. Not yet.

She'd barely had Rocco, a chance at this new life. She was just getting started. "Alex—"

The back door to USD slammed closed.

Rocco.

Alex lifted a finger and pressed it to his lips.

Heavy footfalls came down the hall, Rocco's boots

thudding with each step. That was when a bolt of fear flashed through. Fear for him.

Tears burned at the back of her eyes. She loved Rocco. *Loved* him. And she couldn't let Alex hurt him.

Rocco came around the corner, the smile slipping from his mouth, and stopped cold.

"I want you to watch her die," Alex said, with his back to Rocco, staring at her. "I want you to feel the pain that I feel."

Rocco crept forward, heel to toe, slow and silent.

"Take another step and I'll shoot her in the face." Alex slid his finger to the trigger. "No open casket."

Rocco halted. "But you don't want to kill her. You want her to suffer. You want her to be alone. So, shoot me instead. In front of her. Make her watch me die, slowly, bleeding out and she'll never forget that agony. She'll never dare to fall in love again."

His words gutted her. Because they were true.

To lose Rocco was unimaginable. But in such a horrific way would be unbearable.

Something in her chest cracked and tears welled in her eyes. Alex saw it. That Rocco was right.

He pivoted on his heel, pointing the gun at Rocco.

Adrenaline surged in Mercy. She opened the flap of her handbag.

"Do you want to know why she doesn't love you?" Rocco asked, stalling.

She shoved her hand inside the purse, closing her fingers around the cool grip of steel.

"Why?" Alex asked.

Pulling the SIG out, she flicked off the safety and

took aim at Alex's chest, the way he'd taught her, center mass.

"Because," Rocco said, and she put her finger on the trigger, "you're a weak, simpering coward."

She fired. Blood splattered. She pulled the trigger, again and again until Alex collapsed to the floor.

Rocco ran to her, kicking the gun from Alex's hand along the way. He gripped her shoulders and steered her backward, around the desk and down into the chair. She didn't realize she was shaking until he pried the gun from her hand and put it on the desk.

He picked up the phone, dialed 911 and reported it. As soon as he was done, he knelt in front of her. "It's going to be okay." He took her hands in his and kissed her fingers. "It's over. He's dead. He'll never hurt you again."

She looked down at him. "I'm sorry."

"No, honey. Alex had it coming. There is nothing for you to be sorry for."

Alex had shown her that it was kill or be killed. "I don't regret shooting him to protect you. I'm sorry for endangering you."

"What?" He wrapped his arms around her and held her.

The hug lasted, seconds, minutes, she couldn't tell. But she soaked in his warmth until she stopped shivering.

Rocco pulled back and cupped her face in his hands. "Alex endangered me because he was insane and obsessed with you."

"Exactly. If you had never met me—"

"You've got it all wrong, honey." He kissed the words

from her lips. Her heart beat faster. Not in fear, but at the sheer beauty of how his touch made her feel like being with him was where she belonged. The tears that had been brimming in her eyes fell. But they were tears of relief and love.

She loved him. He loved her. And they'd do anything for each other.

"Meeting you was the best thing to ever happen to me," he said, caressing her cheek and wiping away her tears. "You saved me. Not just by shooting him. But by forgiving me. By loving me." He brought his face to hers until their foreheads touched, and she was lost in the warmth in his eyes. "You saved me in more ways than one."

She thought about her father, the years of his insidious control, and the movement—the cult she'd finally escaped because of Rocco. "I guess we saved each other."

"We did and every day I get to spend with you is worth any danger." He pulled her into another tight hug as a siren wailed, drawing closer.

She sank against him, grateful to be with him, free from her past. They had been through so many trials and had both come so close to dying to get to this point, but she truly didn't have any regrets. She wanted this life, building a future, in love, and safe in his arms, where she belonged.

* * * * *

HARLEQUIN
PLUS

Try the best multimedia
subscription service for romance
readers like you!

Read, Watch and Play.

Experience the easiest way to get
the romance content you crave.

Start your **FREE TRIAL** at
<u>www.harlequinplus.com/freetrial</u>.